The One I Left Behind

PIPER RAYNE

Cover Design: By Hang Le

1st Line Editor: Joy Editing

2nd Line Editor: My Brother's Editor

Proofreader: My Brother's Editor

About The One I Left Behind

It's the classic story—boy goes off into the world to fulfill his dreams and leaves the girl behind.

Not every boy returns home, and I wish Ben Noughton wouldn't have come back to our small ranching town at all after he retired from playing professional football.

I figure it's a quick layover for him. He always wanted out of this town and off his family's ranch. I just have to bide my time until he turns his back on all of us again.

Then he takes on the coaching position for the high school football team and starts milling around too much, bulldozing the protective walls I've built around myself. But he goes too far when he takes my son under his wing to help him be the best player he can be. Leaving me to protect not only my own heart but my son's too.

Because I promised myself a long time ago that I'd never be the girl in the rearview mirror again.

THE ONE I
Left Behind

Chapter One

BEN

The sliding doors of the airport open, and it isn't the Nebraska heat in June that shocks me. Rather, it's my dad and two brothers sitting in an old black pickup truck with the Plain Daisy Ranch logo peeking out from the splatters of dirt along the side.

"It's about fucking time!" Emmett shouts, half his body hanging out the open window of the back seat.

There better be air conditioning in that truck.

My dad isn't an emotional guy, and neither is my older brother, Jude, so I'm surprised they didn't just send Emmett to pick me up from the airport.

My dad rounds the back of the truck and takes my suitcase, tossing it in the back. No pat on the back or hug. We're not very affectionate in the Noughton family.

Dad's presence has a giant red light flashing in my brain. Like those ones above the slot machines to say you won big. Something is wrong. They're treating me too nicely. What's happened since they came out to visit me a couple of months ago when I announced my retirement from football?

"I could've gotten that," I say, opening the door Emmett is hanging out of and shooing him to slide over.

He groans as if he's six and I'm bossing him around, which was a normal occurrence back then. If Jude and I had known that Emmett would grow taller than each of us, maybe we would've held off on razzing him so much. Then again, probably not.

"Welcome home." My dad climbs into the driver's seat of the truck.

The only time we were allowed to drive him around was when we were working on passing our driver's exam. Even then, we'd already been driving on the ranch for years before we turned sixteen.

"Thanks," I mumble.

Excitement isn't the first word I'd use to describe my feelings about returning to my small town. Do I love where I was raised? Hell yeah. Do I love my family? Without question. And I miss the ranch. The cows, horses, all my cousins and aunts and uncles. It might not be Kansas, but as Dorothy said, there's no place like home.

But over the years, I got used to my life in San Francisco. The life of a professional football player who got paid nicely—in dollars and women. People would approach me as if I were God everywhere I went even though I was just playing a sport I loved.

"No AC?" I ask.

Jude scowls over his shoulder. "Have you seen gas prices?"

"Last I heard, the ranch was thriving."

In my fourteen years since leaving the ranch to attend college and go on to play pro, Plain Daisy Ranch turned not so plain. It's a cattle ranch, but with the help of my aunts, uncles, and cousins, they've turned our over five hundred thousand acres into multiple profitable businesses for all.

"It won't be if we waste our money. It's only June, wait until July." Dad glances in the rearview mirror.

He's still got that rugged rancher look. A little scruff as though he hasn't shaved in a few days with a sprinkling of gray and a few deep lines around his eyes, but he still has the fit, lean muscular build under his plaid shirt and jeans from working longer than nine-to-five every day.

I lean my head closer to the window, letting the warm wind blow in my face. We drive out of the city, the tall buildings shifting to corn stalks that aren't quite tall enough to hit your knee. The rolling hills of corn and soybeans lead us toward our town of Willowbrook. I expect to see the rusty old welcome sign with the slogan, "Nothing beats small-town life."

The truck flies past, and I barely catch my name on the new Welcome to Willowbrook sign.

"Did that?" I thumb toward the sign.

Emmett cracks up laughing.

Jude grunts.

Dad straightens up in his seat. "Yep. New sign. You're the best thing to come out of this town, so deservingly so."

I turn to Emmett. "Did it really say home of Ben Noughton, San Francisco Kingsmen?"

He leans in closer, lowering his voice as if Jude and our dad could even hear him over the whooshing wind screaming in through the open windows. "Just wait."

"For?" My eyebrows rise, and he laughs again, shaking his head.

I know better than to ask him twice. This fucker isn't gonna tell me shit.

Other than the sign, nothing has changed. It's still a lot of farms, barns, and fencing with small family homes that have been passed down from one generation to the next. I'm the anomaly of this town. One of the rare ones who got out. The typical story of the country kid who made something of himself.

The farms grow smaller the closer we drive toward our small downtown. And it's not until we reach the outer limits that my body feels as though I'm sinking into quicksand. A slow realization dawns on me when I look at the road ahead. If I thought the sign was bad, this is so much worse.

Dad honks the horn.

Emmett pumps his fist out the window.

Jude shakes his head.

Families are camped out on the sides of the street, chairs, and blankets laid out as if there's a parade. I mentally go through the calendar, hoping for some other option—but it's not the Fourth of July, Memorial Day, or Labor Day. Then I spot it. Mrs. Webster holding up a Welcome Home sign, hand-written with stars that match the cut-outs of her blue-ribbon blueberry pie.

"What the fu—"

Emmett laughs uncontrollably. "It's your welcome home parade!"

I sit up, leaning my head in between Jude and my dad. "A parade?"

"The town wanted to show you how proud they are of you." My dad's grin says he had something to do with this. Probably my aunts—his sisters—too.

"Dad." I whine like I did when I was fifteen and I found my English teacher in the kitchen one morning, wearing my dad's shirt.

"Come on. You're the biggest thing ever to come out of this town. They want to celebrate your accomplishments. What's so bad about that?" Dad parks in the lot of the local grocery store, The Farm Fresh, which always seemed wrong to me since if you really wanted farm fresh, you could visit any of the actual farms in this town.

There are floats and convertibles and flags and giant signs. All with the scarlet red and metallic gold of the Kingsmen.

I groan and sink down in my seat.

Dad turns off the ignition, and he and Jude climb out. My dad immediately strikes up a conversation with someone about the drive to and from the airport.

"Stop acting like a child and get the fuck out of the truck." Jude hits his hand on the door.

Emmett follows suit, and I'm the only one left in the truck until three cheerleaders pop up in front of my window. I startle back and stare at them wide-eyed.

"It's him," the blonde with a giant bow on her head says.

The brunette rolls her eyes. "He's in the truck for Plain Daisy, of course it's him."

The red-haired one creepily stares at me with unblinking eyes.

"Um... hello?" I give them a wan smile.

"I'm Kait." The blonde waves her fingers, grinning.

"And I'm Rey." The brunette takes out her lip gloss, coating her lips before puckering them into a kiss.

Kait points at the red-haired girl. "That's Colette. She's shy."

Colette says nothing.

This is not a good look for me. Three young, impressionable girls corralled around my window as if I'm the only bull on the ranch.

I slide to the other side of the truck. "Nice to meet you all. I gotta go."

I flee the truck before I'm posted on the Canary Wall down at The Hidden Cave. Just when I think I'm free, I run smack dab into Brooks Watson. At least I'm pretty sure it's him. He's changed a lot since he was the quarterback of my high school football team.

"I heard the rumors, but..." I inch back, taking in what I

would've imagined to be a Halloween costume before seeing it on him.

He rests his thumbs in his holster belt. Tattoos and tan skin peek out from under his dark sleeves. "I'm stuck here to make sure your sorry ass doesn't get mauled. Must be tough being a pretty boy now."

His deep chuckle spurs laughter from me because anyone else and I'd probably haul off and hit him, but not Brooks.

I put my hand between us. "It's been a long time."

His hand wraps around mine since we're practically the same size. "Well, you never came back."

We shake hands, and I pocket my hands in my jeans. "I've been back a few times."

I try not to wince at the memory of returning during one Christmas break in college. I'd be lying if I said she hasn't been floating around in my mind more and more lately, knowing I was returning.

"I can still read you like a book." He nods his head to start walking, and I step in line with him. Thankfully, we're not in the thick of Willowbrook residents just yet, so I can catch up with my old friend.

"I have no idea what you're talking about, but Jesus, Watson, a damn parade?"

"Cry me a fucking river. You're king for a day. They'll probably declare today to be Ben Noughton Day." He laughs again, and I'm thankful there's no resentment in his voice.

When I first got accepted to Clemson on a full-ride scholarship, a few of my teammates were upset, wanting their shot. Brooks always stuck up for me, and how did I repay him? By not keeping in touch all these years. Great friend I am.

He puts out his arms when a group of boys try to approach me. "Give Mr. Noughton some space. He's got to go sit on his throne. Autographs afterward."

The boys stare slack-jawed at me, and I shoot them an apologetic smile.

I shake my head. "Hell, Brooks."

"I have to take my job seriously. Protecting Willowbrook's golden boy isn't for the weak."

"Can we cut the crap?"

We end up at a float with a chair that does indeed look like a throne. My dad is huddled nearby with his friends, a huge smile on his face, while Emmett's showing off his dimples to three women. Jude is nowhere to be seen.

"This has to be a joke," I mumble.

"Your chariot awaits." Brooks smacks me on the back.

His booming voice and laughter grab everyone's attention, and the clapping starts, followed by the whistles and hollers and screams.

I can only imagine how red my face is, and it's not because of the sun beating down on me.

"Climb up, son." Dad raises his arm, pointing the way.

Emmett pumps his fist and chants "Ben" over and over. Sure enough, the crowd follows suit, and I have no choice but to climb onto the damn float.

I step onto the wobbly trailer frame, the same one that's used to announce the homecoming king and queen. The same one I've sat on before for that exact purpose, except Gillian was in the chair right next to me. For a second, I'm there again. Her shooting me her soft smile that made my heart soar. Me reassuring her I'd never let her get hurt. I sure broke my promise on that one.

When I sit in the chair, the few people in charge stare at me with accomplished, proud smiles. The truck pulls my trailer behind the marching band playing the high school fight song, heading toward the parade route I know by heart. My eyes look around downtown Willowbrook, with memories at every corner. Right before we hit the crowds, hairs stand up on my arms, and I glance to my left.

She's standing between two trucks in a parking lot. Our eyes catch for the briefest of moments. Her blue eyes capture my complete attention and I lift my arm to wave, but she strips her gaze from mine, turning and disappearing through the parking lot of trucks.

My suspicions were right—this town isn't big enough for the both of us. She can run today, but one day we're going to have to face one another.

Chapter Two

GILLIAN

I slide through the back door, slowly shutting it behind me. "You just couldn't listen to me, huh?"

I turn to find Laurel leaning against the wall with her arms crossed, eyebrows raised above her dark-framed glasses, disappointment lining her face.

"I'm sorry."

She turns to head back into the storefront of her bakery. "I told you that you should've fled town for the day."

I follow her and sit on one of the stools. The bakery and coffeehouse are completely desolate due to the King of Willowbrook's arrival. "I just wanted to catch a glimpse of him. In person."

"And cause yourself more heartbreak?" She puts a smiley face cookie on a plate and slides it over to me.

"The last thing I need is sugar." I push the plate away, but I'm fooling myself. I'm going to eat the cookie and probably a cupcake too.

"Sugar makes the heart hurt less." She rearranges her case of baked goods.

"You should put that on the window." She gives me a

look, and I relent. "I'm not heartbroken. It's been a long time."

She peeks at me under her glasses through the glass case. "But you snuck out to catch a sighting of him?"

"I'm not sixteen sneaking out of my bedroom window. I'm a grown woman who just wanted to see what her ex-boyfriend looked like. It's not that weird."

"Except most women's high school sweethearts weren't professional football players they could watch every Sunday for more than a decade. Not to mention, with this new invention called the internet, you can actually search him." She closes the glass case and puts some cookies in a box that I guarantee she's going to tell me to take home to Clayton.

"Nowadays you can google anyone. I just..."

There's no explanation as to why I didn't stay holed up in Laurel's bakery. I told myself a thousand times to ignore all the hype surrounding Ben's return. That I'd moved on. I told myself I didn't care. They're all lies, though, because I do care.

I swear, the minute his dad's truck rolled past the county line, my throat closed up, and those butterflies I thought had died reemerged. Ben rarely returns to Willowbrook, and the small number of times he has, he has never left their ranch. I'd hear one of his cousins or brothers remark casually about how he'd been home and always in the past tense. Eventually, I became numb to the pain when I realized I wasn't important enough on Ben's list to see. Then again, I can't blame him. Not after all that went down between us.

"Do you think he googled you?" Laurel's eyes light up so bright, my next words almost kill me.

"Have you seen the women he's dated?"

She stops with the purple iced cupcake she was putting in a box in the air and glares. "Don't you dare do that."

I love Laurel. She's a girl's girl. The funny thing is, we weren't that close in high school. She was a cheerleader, and I was... well, not. But we went to the same community college and have been friends ever since.

"I'm not... I'm confident and happy where I am. But thank God we started that kickboxing class this year."

"Gillian." She sighs and shakes her head. She stops what she's doing and rounds the counter before sitting on the stool next to me. "I get it. I do."

Her hand lands on my forearm, and I don't dare look up. I'd rather have her yell at me than this. The pity.

I've been on the receiving end of everyone in Willowbrook's pitying expressions for the past fourteen years.

There's Gillian, the girl Ben Noughton left behind.

Can't believe she actually thought they'd make it.

Can you believe what she did?

I've heard the whispers and the rumors. The first few years were harder than they are now. I think our past moved to the back of people's minds until Bruce Noughton made the big announcement at bingo that his middle son was returning home. Then all the whispers started again. Hell, I'm pretty sure three-quarters of this town thinks Clayton is actually Ben's son.

"Gillian?"

I blink and smile at Laurel, picking her hand off my arm. "I'm good. Fine. I mean... I don't want to talk about it."

She opens her mouth, but the bell on the door rings. We both look, surprised to have a customer while the parade is going on.

"It's ridiculous." My son, Clayton, grabs a chair and sits at a table near the window.

"He's a famous professional football player." Drew, Clayton's best friend, slides the chair out across from him and sits down.

"Hey, boys." Laurel stands and heads back behind the

counter. She grabs two plates and puts cupcakes on them. "Didn't want to be at the parade?"

She puts the plates on their table. Drew picks his up before the plate is barely on the table, takes off the wrapper, and bites down, purple frosting smearing across his lips.

Meanwhile, Clayton stares longingly out the window where the parade should be rounding the corner after it ends to head back to the parking lot of The Farm Fresh.

"Hell no." Clayton sinks in his chair. He looks so big now with his long legs stretched out in front of him. Is that really my baby boy in a fourteen-year-old's body?

"Hey, language," I say.

"Sorry," he mumbles. "It's just... the whole town shuts down for him. And you should see how the girls are all talking about him."

"You're just upset because Kait didn't give you the time of day." Drew piles the last of his cupcake in his mouth, crumbs scattering around his plate and his shirt.

"I don't like Kait."

Drew glances at me from the corner of his eye. We both know Clayton likes Kait. He's had a crush on her since the third grade.

"He is a celebrity of sorts." Laurel brings Drew another cupcake.

"He's not a celebrity," Clay says. "He played football. Probably has that brain disease now."

"Clay..." The warning in my tone should make it clear to him that that's nothing to joke about.

He straightens in his seat. "He's all everyone's talking about."

"Well, who else came out of this town and made it big?" I ask.

"The hype will die down." Laurel glances at me as if she's reassuring the both of us.

"Coach wants us all at The Farm Fresh when the parade is done to meet him." Drew stands from the table just as the marching band reaches Laurel's bakery window.

I don't want to look. I saw him, and now it's over. Except our eyes met briefly, and now I can't stop thinking about those brown eyes that used to look at me as if I hung the moon. As if I were everything to him. But that all changed when he went to Clemson. I naively believed in that look—that we'd be the rare ones to make it work.

"Come on, Clay," Drew says.

My son takes about as long to get up as it does when I ask him to take out the trash. I understand his feelings toward Ben. I'm sure he's heard the rumors around town. He used to love Ben when he was younger. Couldn't believe that a pro player came out of our small town. He used to say he'd go to Clemson just like Ben Noughton. All through it, I'd bite my lip because, to a kid, his mom didn't have a life before he came along.

Something shifted about a month ago, and although Clayton's never asked me outright, he knows. I know he does. How could he not, with the high school still showcasing the prom picture with Ben and me as king and queen? I wish I had the guts to talk to Clay about it rather than what I've been doing, which is ignoring the subject completely. But now Ben is home, and I'm not sure I can put it off anymore.

"If Coach wants you there, go. And be respectful." I raise my eyebrows and tilt my head. It's my serious "mom" look.

He blows out a breath, and Laurel's shoulders sink, watching this play out. Clayton walks over and wraps his arms around me, hugging me. The move surprises me, but I take the opportunity to squeeze him hard because hugs are rare these days. I fear what my life will be like once he's grown and out of the house.

"Are you okay?" he whispers.

There it is. He knows more than any boy should about his mom's broken heart.

"I'm great. Go, and we'll order pizza tonight." I rub his back, and he steps away.

"I'm down for pizza," Drew says, taking the bag of cookies Laurel's holding out to him.

"When aren't you hungry?" Clayton walks toward his friend. "Thanks, Laurel. Bye, Mom."

The door shuts, and once they're out of sight, my forehead falls to the counter. "Oh my god."

"Well, that big secret you were trying to keep is definitely out in the open." Laurel pushes a plate with a cookie on it toward me.

I peek to see her biting the inside of her cheek. "I already knew he knew. I mean, why is that damn prom picture posted in that glass case at the high school anyway?"

"Because it's a Ben Noughton shrine. I'm surprised they haven't erected a brass statue in the town square." She rolls her eyes. "Regardless, you need to talk to him before someone in town spreads false information."

"I know. Tonight."

Her hand lands on my knee and pats it a few times. "It's better if it comes from you."

I nod, although I'm not sure I want him to know exactly how it all went down. There are some things I wish Clayton didn't have to know. The situation with his dad is bad enough. It's like he's nine and I'm telling him there's not really a Santa all over again.

The bell rings on the door, and I groan, not wanting to see anyone from town right now.

"Oh my god, I completely forgot," Laurel murmurs and stands. "Let me go grab it, Mr. Noughton."

I tense up at the name.

"Gillian." Bruce Noughton smiles at me as if it's a regular day. "Just saw your boy. He sprang up fast, huh?"

"Hi, Mr. Noughton. Yeah, he towers over me now."

He sits on the stool next to me. His big build never made me nervous, but that's probably because he's always been polite and shied away from the topic of Ben. But today, something in his face tells me I'm not going to be so lucky. "That's a good thing."

"Definitely." For the first time, I'm forcing a smile with Ben's dad.

He glances out the window, and I glance toward the kitchen, wondering what's taking Laurel so long.

"Hey, we're having a welcome home party... at the ranch... you should come." Bruce takes off his cowboy hat and runs his hands through his hair before putting it back on.

Emmett takes after their mom, at least from the pictures I've seen of her, but Ben and Jude are practically spitting images of Bruce. In the first years after Ben left, it was hard to look at Bruce. And if I saw Jude walking down the street, I'd think for a moment that it was Ben returning.

"Oh, I would love to, but I can't." Normally, for anyone else, I would make up some excuse, but Bruce isn't stupid. His invitation was polite, but we both know I shouldn't be anywhere near the ranch these days.

"Next time." He winks. The Bruce Noughton charm that everyone talks about shines.

"Definitely."

"Here you go." Laurel comes out, holding a huge white box. She sets it on the table, and Bruce rises to his feet.

I don't have the heart to read the words that I'm positive are inscribed on one of Laurel's delicious cakes.

"Looks great as always." Bruce pulls out cash to pay for the cake.

As Laurel checks him out, her gaze keeps diverting in my

direction. Because we both know she could've warned me about this.

"Thanks again. See you two around." Bruce nods, his eyes lingering on me a little longer than Laurel.

I hurriedly rush to open the door for him.

"Thanks, Gillian." He nods.

I continue holding the door open, watching him walk toward the mass of people at the end of the parade.

My gut twists at who is in the center of that crowd. I can't see him, but I know it's him. Signing autographs with that smile that causes my heart to pick up pace. I'm sure he'll be gone soon. And if he isn't, I will be.

BEN

I'm going to kill my dad. After sitting like fucking Santa Claus on a float in the Thanksgiving Day parade for the past twenty minutes waving to the residents of Willowbrook, I now have to sign autographs and shake hands.

And as if it couldn't get worse, my dad disappeared about five minutes ago. He could talk to some of these people or at least say the names I've forgotten.

"Get out of my way," a gruff voice says, and all I see is people parting to make room.

I laugh, handing over a picture of me with a signature on it to the little boy in front of me because I know who that voice belongs to.

"Benny boy." Coach Marks puts out his arms, and I stand, hugging him over the table.

"Coach."

"Just came by to remind you why you're a pro player." He laughs, pointing at himself, and a few people around him do too.

Coach Marks should've been on that float with me. Although his beard is almost completely gray now, and his stomach a little more stretched over his pants, he still has the same gregarious smile.

"You're already getting soft." He pokes my stomach with his finger. "Better hit the gym to keep that shape." His stomach bounces with laughter.

"Can't say it's not something I've been worried about."

I've seen other players who retired, and the muscle mass gets lost when you're not training the way you were while in the league. But whatever my dad has planned for me on the ranch should help.

"Ah, as long as I'm around, I'm not gonna let you get too soft." Coach steps aside, and there's a group of boys behind him, all wearing their Willowbrook High School football jerseys. "The boys want to meet you. Boys, this is Ben Noughton."

They file in line, each one shaking my hand. So many of them remind me of myself at that age. Naïve as to how tough football is once you're out of high school. But most won't see college play. I hate that fact, but it's the truth. Sometimes I wonder how I even got to the pro level.

"I'm Drew. Running back. Freshman." The kid's so excited, his palm is a little clammy. "I'm your biggest fan. Never missed a game. Any advice?"

Coach Marks slaps Drew on the back. "Relax there, kid. Move along." He looks at me. "He's a little hyper, you know?"

"Thanks, Drew," I say, nodding before he gets away.

"Clayton, what're you scared of?" Coach Marks says to the kid, sauntering toward me as if he's on death row walking toward the execution room.

"Sorry, Coach." His voice is low. He must be the shy type. He puts his hand out between us. "Clayton."

Coach Marks glances at me. As I slide my hand into the kid's, I realize a lot of eyes are on me, and all the sounds of people talking turn into hushed whispers.

Oh shit.

Clayton.

"Clayton Adams?" I ask.

His eyes lock with mine, and it's all I can do not to react. How did I not notice when he first approached? He's got Gillian's eyes. The same cornflower blue I stared into so many nights under the stars in the back of my truck.

"Yes, sir." His tone is cold and distant. A vast difference from the kid before him.

"Call me Ben."

He slides his hand out of mine and shoves it in his pocket, walking away toward the group of boys. Obviously the boy hates me, but it's no surprise that Gillian raised him to be polite. I'd expect nothing else.

My vision shifts to Coach, and he's got a look on his face that says, "Yep, that's your high school sweetheart's boy. You really fucked that up." But instead of saying it, he crosses his arms on top of his belly. "How about you assist me this year?"

Fuck, I don't want to coach football. "Um... I'm not sure what my dad has planned for me at the ranch."

His eyes narrow, but he laughs and shakes his head. "You can at least come down and run a few camps. You owe me that much."

"Deal."

"That's what I thought. Now, I'll let these other people get in here to meet the man I developed." He smirks and ambles off, yelling at the boys to go pick up some trash leftover from the parade.

They all groan, but as I once did, they listen and scatter in different directions.

I watch Clayton for a moment, and surprisingly, he looks over his shoulder at me. He's definitely not my biggest fan. That was clear from his cold demeanor. Who can blame the kid? I'd hate the guy who broke my mom's heart too. Then again, if I hadn't, he wouldn't be here.

"Excuse me?" A small voice pulls me away from my thoughts.

A boy around six stands in front of me with a small football in his hands.

"Hey." I sit back down.

He hands me the football, and I continue signing autographs as if it's a publicity event my agent organized.

My hand cramps on the last signature, and my dad comes to sit on the corner of the table. "Ready now?"

I put the cap on the marker. "I was ready when I landed, but you planned this damn thing."

A guy from The Farm Fresh comes over to take down the table, and my dad and I both thank him before walking to his truck. A few lingering residents come over to give me a handshake and say a few words to my dad.

When we reach the truck, it's empty.

"Where're Jude and Emmett?" I ask.

"Jude got a ride back with Sadie, and who knows what happened to Emmett. Probably eight inches into some blonde by now." Dad climbs into the driver's seat, and I see a giant white cake box in the back seat.

I guess the welcome-home party isn't over yet. But a party at the ranch, I'm always down for.

"You're aware of where Emmett gets his ways, right?"

My dad's face crinkles as if I asked him to solve a calculus problem.

"You."

"Me?" He starts the truck and backs out, still looking confused.

"How many times did we wake up to a different woman at our kitchen table wearing your shirt?"

He laughs. "Hardly ever. I usually made sure they were gone before you kids woke up." He winks at me.

I shake my head. "When I came home last year, you brought home some woman you'd met at The Hidden Cave."

"She was an old friend."

"You say they're all old friends."

"They are." He shrugs. "Plus, I don't see you with someone steady on your arm." He turns out of town, waving to a few more people before we're on the country roads.

"I haven't found anyone. I thought there was one woman, but..."

"Xavier Greene's girl?"

I shouldn't be surprised that my dad knows everything. It was years and years ago that I tried to date my quarterback's best friend. Looking back, I think she just reminded me of Gillian. Small-town girl, sweet. The opposite of the jersey chasers. Looked the opposite of Gill, since I mostly go for blondes now instead of brunettes. Something about seeing dark hair strewn across my pillow makes my heart ache. Anyway, Xavier won the girl, as he should have.

"It was over before it started," I say.

"They seem happy. Just saw a piece on them enjoying his retirement years up in Alaska."

I nod, not wanting to get into relationship stuff with my dad, even though I started it. Based on his next words, he doesn't feel the same.

"Speaking of girls from small towns, I saw Gillian today."

And there it is. It took my dad little to no time with us alone to bring her up. Every time I visit, he tries to fill me in on Gillian's life, but I shut him down right away. I'm quite happy not knowing anything, and besides, it's none of my business. Which is why I purposely don't tell him that I saw her too.

"She was at Laurel's bakery. You remember Laurel, right? Those two are tighter than a farmer and his tractor."

I still don't comment.

"She looked a little shaken."

I stare out the window at the neighboring farms zipping past.

"You should reach out to her. Get a drink or coffee. Clear the air now that you're here full time."

"I never said I was here full time. It's a pit stop." Which is what I told myself after I retired and my dad asked me to come home. I'll appease him for a little bit, but this isn't where I want to land. My agent is talking to people about me being an analyst for Sunday games.

My dad frowns, even though this isn't news to him. "Sometimes pit stops turn out to have a lifespan."

"Not this time." I love my family, but I'm not meant for Willowbrook. I don't want the fish fry every Friday, where everyone gossips about what they've seen all week.

"Remember, this town built you. After your mom…"

His voice cracks as it does every time my mom is brought up, which isn't often. He's always quick to tell me he could barely meet our needs after my mom died, and if it wasn't for his sisters and the people of Willowbrook, us boys would've run wild. I hate to break it to him. We kind of did, especially Emmett.

All I remember is Aunt Bette rocking Emmett to sleep for months in the same rocking chair my mom did. Aunt Darla read us bedtime stories, and our fridge and freezer were stocked full of casseroles. Men I barely knew worked the ranch.

"I haven't forgotten."

We pull down the long, winding road toward our property under the big arch that says Plain Daisy Ranch with the horseshoe in the middle, and my mind is flooded with memories.

We're on the east side of the Noughton property, which mostly consists of the cattle ranch. The businesses that my aunts and uncles started are on the west side. There's a big lake in the middle of our property, around which all of the houses are sporadically placed, except for my dad's home. He never wanted to rebuild, staying in the house that he'd built for my mom.

"Smack on a smile because we're having a family party." He parks his truck in front of my family home with the giant porch around it.

"I don't have to fake the smile. I'm happy to see them."

"Good. Enjoy your night, and tomorrow morning, we'll talk about your duties on the ranch. And what kinda house you're gonna want to build."

"My house?"

"Jude and Emmett have moved out, built houses of their own. You need to as well." He opens his door to climb out.

"Can't I just stay in my old bedroom until..." I don't remind him that I'm not staying for the long term.

"You're a grown man, Ben. You shouldn't live in the family house. You can stay until you finish your house."

He's out of the truck and shuts the door. What the hell happened to my welcome home?

As I'm about to ask him another question, the front door opens, and all my family members file out with big smiles and open arms. They swarm me like offensive linemen on a running back with the ball one yard from the goal.

My aunts kiss my cheeks and hug me tight.

My uncles shake hands and give me one-armed hugs.

My female cousins give me tight hugs, each whispering how sorry they were about the parade but that I was a trooper.

My guy cousins all razz me about how red my face was and how the king has returned.

Jude looks disgruntled on the porch, sitting with Sadie at his side.

I wish I had time to walk the ranch and visit our oldest

cow, Bessie, but that would be ungrateful to my family and the planning they did.

"Don't you all have businesses to run?" I ask the group.

They laugh, and some of my family walks back into the house, while others head around to the circle of chairs set up around the fire pit.

Now this is something I missed. A relaxing night with my family, talking shit.

A short time later, I have a beer in my hand, and my cousin Romy approaches me. "So, did you see her? Rumor has it she was hiding out with Laurel at the bakery."

My cousin is a romantic at heart, which is probably why she works at The Knotted Barn, the barn that's been converted into a wedding chapel and reception venue. She's single and hasn't found her one yet, but she's always looking. So, I'm not surprised she wants to talk about Gillian. To her, it's probably a reunion written in the stars. But our history was penned a long time ago, and I don't see a reprint ever happening.

Chapter Four

GILLIAN

I open the screen door. "Thanks, Ned."

He gives me the pizza, and I hand him money. Usually, the man is quick to rush off and deliver his next pizza, but tonight he hems and haws under the star-filled Nebraska sky.

"Did I not give you enough?" I ask. My mind hasn't been where it should be today.

"No, you did. I was just wondering if you were okay."

Oh, for fuck's sake. Not Ned, my shy pizza delivery guy who usually takes the money and is off my porch before I even shut the door.

"I'm good." I put on my best smile.

"Okay," he mumbles and turns to head off the porch.

"Thank you for asking, though." I rush out the words before he gets too far away. The politeness my mother taught me at a young age before she passed is still ingrained.

I love Willowbrook, but sometimes everyone being in everyone's business is too much.

"Finally. I'm starved." Clayton takes the pizza from me, then lifts his hand. "Hey, Ned."

Ned nods and climbs into his truck.

"Why doesn't he talk much?" Clayton asks, walking into the kitchen.

I shut the door and follow him. "He's been like that since high school. I hate to use the word shy because I've known him since I was in kindergarten, but he still doesn't say a lot."

"Really? He never got comfortable with you?"

I shrug. "I guess not."

I reach into the cabinet to grab two plates while Clayton pours himself a pop and gets me a bottle of water.

Opening the box, Clayton leans forward and inhales the smell of the cheeseburger pizza. "You should've gotten two." He places two slices on his plate and grabs his pop, heading toward the family room.

"I thought maybe we could eat at the table tonight."

He stops and circles around. "Why? It's summer break."

I'm not sure what summer break has to do with why he shouldn't have to sit at the table for dinner, but I gave up trying to read a teenager's mind a long time ago.

I place my slices on my plate and shake my head. "I just thought it would be nice."

He walks over to the small kitchen table that seats four, with no room for more. We don't get a lot of guests except for Laurel and Drew. After my dad passed, we had my brother and sister here for a while, but Koa and Briar were able to attend college thanks to my dad's life insurance money, so they don't live here anymore.

Pulling out the chair, he positions himself so he can still watch the television from his seat. I turn off the television and sit across from him.

"Just tell me," he says, leaving his pizza untouched on his plate.

"It's nothing big. Start eating."

Clayton leans back in his seat and stares at me. "What? Are we moving?"

I hate that he overheard my conversation a month ago with a company in Lincoln that was interested in me if I passed the bar this summer. "No... I mean, not at this moment."

He purposely looks away. I know his stance on moving, but he's only a freshman, and he'll make friends wherever we go. But I'm not going to get into that conversation again.

"Come on, Mom, I hate it when you're so serious and wanna have a talk. I don't have a girlfriend. I know you and Drew think I like Kait, but I don't."

I sip my water, buying myself some time. "It's about Ben Noughton."

His shoulders stiffen and his back straightens like a dog's response to a possible intruder. "What about him?"

My head tilts. "I know you know."

"It's kind of hard not to. I mean, you've lived in Willowbrook your entire life, so I'm not sure why you thought I never would."

I had hoped for more time, but he has a point. I waited too long. "I'm sorry for that."

"Do you know what it was like when I saw that picture? We toured the high school at the end of the year, and there was a picture of you and him next to his letterman jacket and pictures of him in his uniform."

This is my Clayton. He may have waited for me to bring up the topic, but he's not going to hold back from telling me everything he's feeling now that it's out in the open.

"I should've mentioned it earlier."

"You let me wear his jersey and walk around town telling people how I wanted to be him one day." He takes a big bite of his pizza since he's a stress eater, just like me. With a mouth full of food, he says, "How embarrassing. I was idolizing my mom's ex and didn't even know it."

"It's not embarrassing. You were a kid, and everyone in this town thinks highly of Ben."

"Still, Mom..." I give him my "mom" look so he'll stop talking with his mouth full, and he swallows. "It felt like everyone knew and I didn't. I was a joke. People probably laughed behind my back."

I lean back in my chair. "That's not true, Clay. During football season, you can't go a block without hearing someone say something about Ben. You were taught to love him."

There was a time I selfishly wished that Ben wouldn't have made it so big. That he wouldn't have been so famous. Not because I didn't want him to succeed or because I wanted him to have to come back to Willowbrook, but because it would've made my life easier. I would've left town myself after everything went down, but who would've watched after Koa and Briar?

"Now my friends keep telling me the stories their parents are telling them." He finishes his piece of pizza and guzzles down some pop. "Mom..."

He fiddles with his other slice of pizza. He's definitely contemplating his next question, and my heart rate picks up because if it is what I think it is, that means he's heard the rumors. The untruthful ones.

He lifts his head and sets his gaze on me. "Is he my dad?"

Clayton has asked about his dad a lot, and I've always said he was long gone when I found out I was pregnant. That I tried to reach him and never heard back.

"No. He's not."

"Holden Epstein said his dad told him he was." He picks up his pizza and eats.

"I would've told you if he was. Plus, Ben would've taken responsibility." That, I know, is true. I get the gossip, though. I've never been forthcoming about who Clay's father is, just that it isn't Ben.

"So, then why try to keep it a secret from me that you two dated?"

"I guess you're old enough now to understand." I take a moment to collect my thoughts. "I was embarrassed after it didn't work out with Ben. We were the 'it' couple people thought would make it. Everyone assumed we'd get married and have ten kids, myself included. Within weeks of him leaving for Clemson, I felt the strain between us. He was on to bigger and better things, and I wasn't. I was here, helping to raise Uncle Koa and Aunt Briar while Grandpa worked. We ended up fighting on our phone calls more than talking, and eventually we had no choice but to admit to ourselves that it wasn't going to work. I was devastated."

"And then you slept with whoever my father is?"

I nod. "Yeah." I debate for a second whether I should tell him more, but he's almost fifteen. I think he can handle it. "I was at a bar outside of town one night, and a guy gave me a lot of attention. We commiserated together about being the ones left behind. Him for reasons different than mine, but we understood what the other was feeling. He left the next day."

"So, he doesn't even know about me?"

This is where it gets tricky. How do I tell Clayton that his father did know about him, but it didn't matter? I can't hurt him like that. So, I lie. "I sent him a text message. Asked him to call me. He never did. Maybe he changed his number or something. I tried again, and the number was disconnected."

Waylon Knight didn't like responsibility, and I was one of a long list of women he'd slept with. He ran away from town and hasn't returned since.

Clayton stands to get more pizza, piling his plate high with three more pieces. I watch him from my seat. His shoulders are curved in, his eyes only on his task. He's processing, so I let him think for a moment.

Sitting back down, he looks at me. "Thanks for being honest."

His words are a knife in the heart. I just can't bear to tell him that his dad knows he exists and doesn't care. That he didn't want a relationship with Clay. He's a great kid, and I've always tried to be enough. In the end, Waylon leaving town saved us both a lot of trouble.

I nod and pick up my pizza.

"Do you regret it? Sleeping with my dad?" He smirks, knowing the answer already. Clayton is too smart a boy not to know the answer.

"Well, not until you turned thirteen." I grin at him, and he throws a piece of crust at me. "Hey now, don't start a food fight." I throw it back at him and hit him right on the forehead.

"I think I got my arm from you." He sets the crust on the table.

"I never played a sport, but I like to think I'm athletic. Raising you improved my skills."

Clayton was the kind of boy who had to do every single sport, even down to hip-hop dance. He settled on football. I'm not sure if that's because it's what this town is all about and he felt pressure, or if he really loves the sport.

"How about you tell me about Kait?"

He picks up his plate and heads into the kitchen, giving me my answer. "Mind if I go play video games?"

"Well, I'm here if you want to talk about anything."

He walks over and wraps his arms around me from behind. "Thanks, Mom."

I hold his arms, not wanting him to let go just yet. "You know you're the best thing in my life, right?"

He chuckles and steps back. "I know. I'm awesome."

He heads to his bedroom, and I finish eating my pizza alone

at the kitchen table. Now that Clayton is older, I find myself alone a lot. Even with my busy schedule of work and studying for the bar exam, I'm discovering what my life might look like after Clayton graduates. And it's a little lonely, if I'm honest.

I clean up the pizza and wipe down the table, the television beckoning me to watch one of the reality TV shows I love to binge, but there's another pull inside me after today. Though I'm not sure why I enjoy torturing myself.

Lifting onto my tiptoes, I grab the box from the shelf in my closet. The box I should have burned a long time ago. I sit on my bed, for once thankful to overhear Clayton screaming at his friends about the game they're playing because it gives me some privacy.

My hands tremble slightly as I open the lid of the box. It's all there, as it was the last time I looked. Small notes Ben gave me in high school, either left in my locker or handed to me when we'd pass in the hallway. My corsage from prom, my prom queen sash. All the items that spur memories of my time with Ben. Pictures of us so young and naïve, thinking we'd found the love of our lives at such a young age. Last, the letters he'd written me while at Clemson. The scribbled love yous above his name.

My phone dings on the bed next to me with a text message.

Put away the box.

I set it all aside.

You're scary.

No, I just know you. And I would've done the same.

> Tell me why my anger toward him has waned since he returned.

That I don't know. I'd be at Plain Daisy Ranch beating his ass.

I've hated Ben but yearned for him all at the same time. Yearned for the love we'd shared. Yearned for the connection I've never found with anyone else. But I'll never tell him any of that. And I certainly won't let anyone hurt me like that again.

Chapter Five

BEN

I squint at the sun coming through one small crack in the blinds. Rolling over, I grab my phone, seeing that it's only seven o'clock. Although everyone else is probably already up and working the ranch, my dad said I start this afternoon because he has stuff for me to do this morning. In fact, there's a text message from him, probably giving me my marching orders.

> 9:00 Dr. Whitaker.

He's got to be joking. I'm a thirty-two-year-old man. I can schedule my own dental visits, so I hammer a text back.

> I'm not going to the dentist.

> You are.

> I'm not.

> You probably have a mouthful of cavities.

I don't.

Want to bet?

Ugh, my dad and his bets. It's how he always gets us to do shit.

I'm too old to play your games.

I was going to offer to make my burgers and fries tonight if you were cavity-free.

You're lying.

But since you're not going to the dentist, thanks for saving me a trip to the store. I'll defrost the liver.

I'm not seven.

Gotta go cancel Dr. Whitaker now.

I toss my phone on my bed, fully aware of the game my dad is playing. But I've been gone a long time, and now that my dad's mentioned his juicy burgers with homemade cut fries, there's no way liver will satisfy me tonight. He's so aggravating.

I pick the phone back up.

I'm going. Happy?

No but you will be when you don't lose all your teeth by the time you're fifty.

I fling the bedspread off and sit to rest my feet on the floor.

Last night, I drank a little too much with my cousins, and by the time I got to my room, all I wanted was my bed.

Now I'm taking in my childhood room that looks the same as the day I left for college. The trophies and stupid posters of expensive cars. The blank corkboard above my desk from when I came home the first time and took down every single reminder of Gillian. The memories were too painful. Not that they don't still haunt me. The worst is that I can almost feel her in this room. The first time we had sex was on my bed when my dad was out of town buying cattle. Jude had gone with him, and Emmett was at my aunt's.

Not wanting to remember any of that, I head out of my room and into the bathroom. The house is quiet since my dad is gone and my brothers have their own houses now.

"Hey, Milo," I say as I pass my dad's room.

The elderly golden retriever picks up his head for a second and lays it back down at the end of my dad's bed. He doesn't even go run around the ranch while my dad's working anymore.

While the water warms up, I brush my teeth, inspecting them as if I could see if I have a cavity. Then I step into the small-ass tub shower where the showerhead is pretty much level with my head. I miss my walk-in shower out west.

The water streams down over me, and the memory of my first time with Gillian rushes back. Her fearful but trusting eyes as I slowly undressed her. We'd fooled around so much by then that it wasn't my first time seeing her naked. I can't help but wonder how her body would feel like now. Then my mind wanders to seeing her yesterday—her long, dark hair and a few more curves.

I soap my body, and my hand slides down to my dick, tugging it a few times. That's all it takes. In one swift motion, I'm back on my childhood bed with Gillian riding me. Her tits bounce, and my fingers dig into her hips. Her cheeks flushed pink, her teeth biting down on her lip, and her eyes full of lust. Lust for me.

I fist my dick and place my free hand on the plastic wall of the shower. Goddamn, it hasn't felt this good in a long time. Her hair slides back and forth, and I deny myself the urge to grab it and wrap my fist around it. Her hands are on my chest in order to keep control, and I raise my hips off the bed to get as deep as I can.

She's warm and wet, and my dick slips in and out as she rises and falls on top of me.

My fist moves faster, and my hand flexes on the wall, wishing I had something to grab on to.

She closes her eyes and falls down on me, her lips crashing to mine, and that's when I take control. My hand slides into her hair, pulling as I devour her mouth. She moans and clenches around my dick. I flip her over and drill in and out of her until my own wave of pleasure washes over me.

I come so hard that I rest my forehead on the shower wall, breathing heavily and processing what I just did. I've masturbated to Gillian a lot over the years, but seeing her yesterday made it so much more intense.

"Stop!" The bathroom door whips open.

My head flies up off the shower wall. Seconds later, the toilet seat hits the back of the toilet.

"What the fuck, Emmett?"

"Didn't mean to interrupt your beat-off session. Aunt Darla poisoned me with her potato salad last night."

"Get out!" I shout.

"Too late for that."

I whip the curtain open to find my brother sitting on the can. His eyes zero in at my dick.

I yank a towel off the rack and wrap it around myself. "Stop looking."

"You're at eye level."

I step out of the shower to get the hell out of here. "I'm sure there are other bathrooms in this house. Or better yet, I'll bet you have some at your place. Why the hell are you in mine?"

"It's *ours*. Just because you're staying here doesn't mean it's *yours*. And I do my best work here."

"You're sick." I walk out the door and into the hall.

"Don't worry, women say size doesn't matter." He cackles.

"Fuck off!" I slam my bedroom door shut, closing off Emmett's laughter.

⸙

DR. WHITAKER'S OFFICE IS IN DOWNTOWN Willowbrook, so I park my dad's truck in one of the angled parking spots and walk down three storefronts to where his name is on the window. I fucking hate the dentist.

The bell rings, and a bunch of magazines lower, searching out who just came in. I lift my hand and wave, scanning the group. A set of blue eyes stops me from continuing in. Our gazes lock and hold, just as they did yesterday.

Well, shit, I guess it's time to take the plunge. We're going to be circling one another with how small this town is.

First, I approach the receptionist behind the counter.

"Welcome home, Benny," she says, her long fingernails typing on the keyboard.

"Hi, Mrs. Fortmeyer. Ready to win the chili contest at the state fair again?"

"You know it." Her pink lipstick is stained on her front tooth. "I checked you in. Have a seat."

I glance at the packed room full of people and back to her. "How long is the wait?"

"Oh, not too long." She smiles sweetly.

I plaster on a fake smile and imagine biting into that juicy burger tonight.

I look around and swallow a laugh because someone has to be messing with me. Is Emmett here? The only chair available is right next to Gillian, and it's not even two seats. It's one of those double chairs with no bar to separate us.

I walk over and signal to the empty spot next to her. She slides over, clutching her purse as if she's on a New York City subway at one in the morning. To her, I am probably as bad as a thief who goes after innocent people.

"Thanks."

My thigh brushes against hers. I glance down to see she's wearing a dress, her legs are crossed, and a lot of her tanned skin is showing. I inwardly groan, and my hand grips my knee. My shower session comes to mind, and now I'm half-hard in my pants.

All eyes are on us. I don't look up, but I can feel them.

I shift to get more comfortable, and our arms brush against one another's. She makes a noise and turns so her back is half faced away from me.

There's no way I can sit here and not say anything.

"How are you?" I ask in the lowest voice I can manage. It doesn't matter how quiet I am, everyone around us is going to hear.

One woman scoffs, and Gillian's attention shifts to her before returning to me.

Without looking at me, Gillian answers politely, "I'm great. And you?"

"I'm okay."

"So, what did your dad bet you?"

I smile because she knows me so well. "If I don't have cavities, he's making his burgers and fries for dinner."

"And if you do?"

"Liver."

She half huffs, half laughs. "I hope you have a cavity then."

"Just one?"

"Now that you mention it, I wouldn't mind if you needed a root canal. Maybe a tooth extraction. Do you still have your wisdom teeth?"

"I do."

"Then wisdom teeth removal without anesthesia."

I nod. "I figured."

The bird-watching magazine Mr. Patel is reading shakes from his laughter.

"I met Clayton." I continue the conversation for reasons I don't understand, except that it's been too long since I heard her voice. It's matured a little over the years, but it still holds that same sweetness that drew me to her the first time.

"Was he polite?"

"Of course."

She nods. "Good."

"Why would you think he wouldn't be?"

"He's not your biggest fan."

"He used to be. Remember when he used to run all over town saying he wanted to be Ben Noughton?" Mr. Patel says and Mrs. Miller elbows him for his comment.

I smile, thinking about Gillian buying my jersey for her kid.

"That was a long time ago." Gillian is quick to respond. "He much prefers Damon Siska with the Chicago Grizzlies now."

I react as she wants, and a sound erupts out of me that confirms to her that she hit her mark. Of course, she's smart enough to pick the kid who was rumored to be a contender to replace me but ended up staying with his team because the Kingsmen traded for Brady Banks instead.

For the first time, she looks at me. "Oh wait, you two play the same position, right?"

"Yeah."

"I guess that happens. People start to follow the younger guys."

"Bull's-eye," I whisper, and she giggles.

"I do love Damon Siska," Mrs. Miller says. "When you played against him this year, Benny, he was all over the field. That safety of yours, Miles what's-his-name, couldn't stop him."

"I watched that game too," Mr. Patel interrupts. "You should tell that Miles fella he needs to be faster."

Gillian laughs, and when my eyes cut to hers, she sucks her plump pink lips in to stop herself. She mouths, "Sorry," but her facial expression says she's anything but.

"I'll be sure to tell him. We all love Monday morning quarterbacks. They're a wealth of knowledge."

"Glad I could help." Mr. Patel lifts his magazine, and I shake my head.

"Benny, you really should pay it back and help Coach Marks with the football team this year." Mrs. Miller starts a new conversation when I just want to be called back and get this appointment over with.

"Who's the dental hygienist now?" I ask, changing the topic.

"Dr. Whitaker's daughter, Missy. She just graduated from hygiene school." Gillian smiles. "Actually, isn't it her first day, Mrs. Miller?"

Mrs. Miller's forehead crinkles. "I think you're right, Gillian. He put up that big sign last week to say they had more openings for patients."

Holly, Dr. Whittaker's hygienist ever since I was a kid, comes out the door from the back. "Gillian, I'm ready for you."

Gillian pats my knee and stands. "I always have Holly. She just knows my teeth so well. You know, because I've lived here my entire life. Enjoy the liver tonight." She says it all without her sweet smile faltering.

A girl who looks as if she just stepped out of high school accidentally bumps into Holly. Holly jolts forward, and Gillian grabs her arms to hold her steady.

"Oh sorry. I'm so clumsy." The girl looks at the chart in her hands. "Benjamin... Noughton? OMG. I'm going to clean Ben Noughton's teeth?"

I stand, and her mouth hangs open.

"It appears that way." Every instinct inside me says to run and run fast.

"I can't wait to tell my friends. Do you mind if we take a picture? Oh... I have to post this, like, now."

Gillian places her hand on Missy's arm. "Missy, Ben likes his teeth pearly white. You know all the photos he takes, he doesn't want any yellow stains, so make sure you really get in there and remove all the plaque and buildup." She glances over her shoulder at me. "Welcome home, Noughton." Then she disappears through the door, following Holly.

"Ready?" Missy asks with a huge grin.

Mr. Patel lowers the corner of his magazine. "Better you than me," he whispers.

Burger and fries. Burger and fries.

Chapter Six

GILLIAN

Clayton has Drew over tonight, so I decide to go to the library to study for the bar exam. It's only held twice a year in Nebraska, and I really want to pass it so I can finally start my law career.

I walk in, and Mr. Torres smiles up from his computer at the reception desk.

"Gillian. Burning the midnight oil again?" He lowers his reading glasses and rubs his eyes.

"Hi, Mr. Torres. Only for a few more weeks." I lift my hand and cross my fingers.

His long salt-and-pepper hair shifts when he shakes his head. "You have this in the bag, and then you can represent everyone in Willowbrook."

I smile politely, not telling him that practicing law in Willowbrook isn't really part of my dream. I want the big cases in a big city where people don't know my past.

"We need a town lawyer instead of everyone going over to Hickory."

"Yeah," I agree, not really wanting to get into this topic.

"Well, have at it. I need to start my restocking. If the book club in the back gets too loud, let me know." He winks.

"Thanks, Mr. Torres."

He puts a sign on his desk that says to ring the bell and walks away from his desk, pushing the cart full of books people returned or decided against.

I head to my favorite spot in the corner behind a row of architecture books, hoping no one will see me and I can get some studying in.

I've barely begun when the book club discussion in the back grows louder. I lean back in my chair to hear better, and it's clear they're definitely not talking about a book. These days, I'm not part of the gossip, but with Ben's return, I've found myself more worried about gossip containing me and Clayton.

"I never thought he'd come back. I thought for sure he'd find some model, marry her, and have kids," a man says. I think it's Mr. Schmidt, the town butcher.

"He was dating that one woman, but I heard that crashed and burned. Maybe he can't commit because he still wants Gillian." The woman's voice is laced with hope.

"Oh... do you think he's here to win her back?" another woman asks.

I roll my eyes. Even if he was, I hate to break it to them, but I'm not game for another round. Of course, they assume that little sweet Gillian, who got her heart broken, would run right back into Ben's arms.

"This isn't one of your romance books. Jeez, Louise," Mr. Schmidt says.

"There's nothing wrong with romance books. They give hope to us women who have to deal with the likes of men like you."

I want to raise my fist and cheer for Louise.

"Can we just get back to the book discussion now?" a woman interrupts before Louise and Mr. Schmidt go at it.

"I was merely saying that the man is probably gonna be a Hall of Famer one day. He isn't going to stick around Willowbrook. This town has never been big enough for him."

My heart twists and squeezes, hearing the truthful words from Mr. Schmidt. Ben was always destined for more than what this town could offer him.

"Sometimes your heart speaks so loud you give up on things like careers and money," says a woman who I think is Louise from the city clerk's office.

"Not as much money as that kid made. Plus, there's rumors he might be a TV analyst on Sundays," Mr. Schmidt says.

I heard the same rumors. Ben isn't a sit-around-and-wait-to-see-what-comes-his-way kind of guy. He's not going to do nothing. He probably already has his second dream job in mind.

"Money and prestige don't keep you warm at night," a new woman's voice says.

"No one cares about that stuff when you die." A man this time. "It's who you are that matters."

"Can we please get back to the book?" the same woman as before asks.

"We all know he regrets leaving her behind."

"Louise, Gillian Adams and Ben Noughton are not characters in your romance novel. He left her high and dry. Either she was pregnant with his baby or she cheated."

My mouth opens at the one rumor I hadn't heard yet. I cheated? Me? The one who stayed here and pined for him. Not the one who had girls giggling in their room. I push up from the chair about to confront the gossiping book club, but I sit back down.

44

"Oh, fuck it," I murmur to myself and stand.

I walk around the two rows of books, pretending I'm looking at some book about Franklin Lloyd Wright. Hey, maybe Clayton has some project for school. They don't know.

"Oh, Gillian," Louise says.

I turn to the group, trying to pretend I didn't overhear them discussing my life.

"Red suits you," she says, gesturing to my shirt, which at the moment matches most of their faces.

The entire group of six have red cheeks, and some of them are even looking at their paperbacks in their laps instead of me.

"Thank you." I pretend to grab a book. "What's the book this month? Surely not a romance book."

Louise glances at Mr. Schmidt, who looks unfazed by my surprise visit.

"Good God, no," Mr. Schmidt says. "Louise has a separate book club for *those* books."

I bite down hard when he refers to romance books as *those* books. As if she should be ashamed of what she's reading.

"It's a mystery novel," Louise says.

"Oh, maybe after I'm done with the bar exam, I can join you guys."

"We're always looking for more people," she says.

"Good." I step forward, keeping my eyes on Mr. Schmidt, but say to Louise, "Although I do like romance, so maybe I'm more suited for the other book club."

Louise smiles as though she just beat out Mrs. Fortmeyer's chili at the state fair. Those two have been competing for years.

I turn to leave but circle back. "Oh, you know what I love to read about? Books that take place in small towns where people gossip about others. Those are some of my favorites."

Mr. Schmidt still looks unfazed, but embarrassment washes over the faces of the other book club members. I didn't say it to embarrass anyone, but I want to shut this down for my son's sake.

Damn Ben for coming home.

I shift to go back to where I was working, but a big body comes through the front door with a stack of books in his arms. Seriously? How can I squash the gossip when he keeps appearing wherever I am?

"Benny!" Mr. Schmidt bellows.

Mr. Torres comes by with his cart in perfect timing. "This is a library, Gary."

The damage has been done. Ben stops at the desk and turns around. I'm standing there like an idiot, watching him when I should be running.

Our eyes catch. I'm really tired of my body's reaction when he looks at me. As if he's apologizing with his eyes.

I take the book I was pretending to read and disappear into my corner. Whatever he's doing here, he won't be long. Ben never was a guy for the library unless he was seeking me out and trying to pry me away.

I open my book and read the same paragraph probably five times because my head is now full of distractions. At this point, I would've gotten more done at home with Clayton and Drew screaming at their friends while playing video games.

"Hey, Gillian." Ben's deep voice causes shivers to scatter along my spine.

Why is he seeking me out? Wasn't I clear at Dr. Whitaker's office that I want nothing to do with him?

I slam my book closed and swivel in my chair. "Noughton, surprised to see you in a library."

He grabs the back of the chair at the desk next to me.

He better not think he's going to sit down.

Sure enough, he slides the chair back and folds his big body into it. "I only ever came here to see you."

"Cute." My tone is one of boredom with the hope he gets the point. He can come home and be everyone's hero, but he's not mine.

"Bennett asked me to return Wren's books. I guess they were past due or were going to be."

Bennett is one of Ben's many cousins, and Wren is his cute six-year-old daughter. Since he's a single dad, I'm sure he needs help. Now I feel as though I can't be mean since Ben's helping out a fellow single parent.

"Jeez, Gill." His brown hair shakes with his head, and his gaze falls to the floor. "I just want to clear the air with you."

Rustling sounds emerge from behind the rows of books.

Oh hell no.

I stand, my chair sliding back, and pack up my books, shoving them into my bag as quickly as I can. "I need to go."

"Wait."

He stands right as I'm about to pass, and I bump into his chest, faltering back a few steps. He grabs my arms, and I push them out of his grasp, stepping farther back. His head tilts, and he studies me for a beat longer than normal.

Before he can say anything, I barrel through the sliver of an opening between him and the bookcase. "Don't follow me."

He doesn't listen. He never listens. I feel him behind me and hear his thundering footsteps a few feet back.

"Bye, Mr. Torres," I say, waving and not making eye contact.

He doesn't say anything because I'm sure he notices my new stalker, and he's unsure how to handle the situation.

The alarm sounds as I pass through the security area. Now I realize why Willowbrook installed them. Because of people like me. There was a big fight when they did, with some town residents feeling offended that the librarians were accusing them of being thieves. Even though the librarians had proof of how many books were disappearing. Now I look like one of those people.

I blow out a breath, turn around, and again smack right into Ben. My eyes fly past his impressive chest and thick neck that I used to kiss and nuzzle my head into. I ignore his soft pink lips that kissed me with love one moment and pure lust the next. Once I meet his eyes, I ignore the questions and the concern.

"Seriously, can you just not?" I push past him and toss my bag on the table in front of Mr. Torres.

Mr. Torres's hands slide along the sides of his head, moving his hair into a ponytail and releasing it. The same nervous tic he does when Miss Greta comes in to read Story-time to the kids every Saturday afternoon. One day, he'll man up and ask her out. I hope.

I dig out the book on bugs that I never should've had in the first place. "I'm sorry."

Mr. Torres accepts the book with a pitying look, obviously feeling bad for me. I'm so done with that look. "Have a good night." He stares past me at Ben.

I walk through the security panels again, and this time, the alarms don't go off. I catch all the book club people staring at me, and it's all I can do not to flip them off.

Once I'm outside with the sun setting, I turn and face Ben. His hands are shoved into the pockets of his shorts, and he looks like a puppy who just got kicked.

"Listen, I get that you're home, but can we just not do this?"

"I wasn't following you," he says.

"For however long we're both in this town together, can we please just move around one another without conversation or pleasantries?"

He steps closer to me. "Answer one question for me."

"No." I flip around, my bag of books swinging around with me.

Ben grunts. "Fuck."

Normally, I'd apologize for hitting someone. But I keep on walking toward my car. He deserves it. I would have gladly taken that physical pain over the heartache and agony he caused me.

Chapter Seven

BEN

I open the door to The Hidden Cave after my run-in with Gillian. The dark bar is half crowded, a few people are sitting on the saddle seats lining the bar, while most are at one of the tables with friends.

I go outside where Brooks told me he'd be. There's a small stage where they have live bands during the summer months, along with lines of picnic tables and a cut-out from a silo that's been made into a circular bar. There are bartenders, but no waitresses. It's a get-your-own-drink-and-find-a-seat kind of place.

"Benny!" Brooks shouts and raises his hand. He's got a group around him, but as I draw closer, I realize he's at a table with my two cousins, Lottie and Romy.

"Girls," I say, kissing each of them on the cheek with a side hug.

"Great, Ben's here, so bye-bye Brooks." Lottie waves at him, picking up her beer and concentrating on Romy.

"What am I missing?" I ask, stealing Romy's beer. She tries to take it back, but I hold her wrist with my hand and take a sip. Gillian has me messed up in the head, and I need a drink.

"You're not missing anything. It's girls' night," Lottie says.

I slide in and bump Romy's hip with mine. She huffs but doesn't fight me. "Well, as your cousin who just got back to town, I'm gonna have to end girls' night."

Lottie glances at Brooks. "Only if you tell me if what's on the wall is true?"

The three of them laugh.

I'm the only one in the dark, but I have a good guess. "Please say you're shittin' me."

Lottie shakes her head, about to spit out her beer.

"Go have a look," Romy says with a smile.

I groan and stand because I'm a curious fucker.

"I'll go with you for moral support." Brooks stands and claps me on the shoulder. "Then we'll get some shots in you."

"That bad?" I turn around, but Brooks pushes me forward.

There are two walls in The Hidden Cave. Canary Wall one and Canary Wall two. Canary Wall one is inside, and you have to submit your gossip cards to an employee who puts them up under glass so that no one can take them down and rip them to shreds. Canary Wall two is outside and more anonymous because it doesn't have the glass casing. It's a post located right next to the silo bar, and Melvin, the owner's son, has long been a permanent fixture at the end of the bar. Which is what's led to the beer belly stretching his blue jean overalls.

"Hey, Melvin," I say, approaching the wall and ignoring all the rest of the eyes on me.

"Benny, heard you were back. One day you have to come and sit next to me and tell me what it's like outside of Willowbrook." Melvin stares at the board then me, raising his bushy dark eyebrows.

Melvin will probably never leave Willowbrook. He's unmarried and sits at the bar almost every night, talking to anyone who approaches him. He's turned into a therapist of sorts from what Emmett told me a few years ago.

Brooks sits down next to Melvin. "The poor guy forgot what it was like here." He laughs and asks the bartender for two shots of whiskey and a beer for me.

One good thing about retirement is I don't have to worry about my weight. No one but me cares if I gain twenty pounds or lose ten anymore.

"The notes have been coming in hot. Just like the old days, you and Gillian are the hot topic," Melvin says.

I scan all the three-by-five cards written in an array of different handwriting. From girly script to men's scribble, each one divulges gossip about someone in town. Originally, the Canary Wall was only used for newsworthy events. Things like the Turner family welcomed a new bull. Or if a road was going to be closed for road work. Maybe someone lost their cat. It was a way to get the word out. But at some point when I was younger, it turned into pure gossip. Although everyone says they hate it, it doesn't stop anyone.

I find the card about me front and center.

I saw Gillian run away from Ben in The Farm Fresh parking lot after they stared at each other for at least three minutes. I think the old feelings only wilted. With a little water (a.k.a. groveling from Ben), maybe their love can sprout again!

"I DON'T GET WHY PEOPLE FEEL THE NEED TO WRITE this shit. Who cares if we saw one another while I was on a fucking float?" I sit on the other side of Brooks and don't wait to cheers him before I down my shot then grab my beer.

"This town doesn't have anything to gossip about that doesn't involve some sort of love connection except for how the Crawfords got all their money after they've been dirt poor forever." Melvin pushes his empty glass over to a blonde bartender I'm not familiar with.

She grabs the glass and fills it for him without a word.

"Last week, someone said the Crawfords won the lottery and have piles of cash buried on their property because they don't want to deposit it for fear everyone in town will know and have their hands out," Brooks says.

"Why can't these people learn to leave people alone?" I sip my beer.

"Hey, hotshot, not all of us were in San Francisco, living it up with celebrities and models." Brooks puts up his fingers for two more shots and looks at Melvin, but he shakes his head. "Two."

"I don't need any more," I say, finishing my beer.

"You sure about that?" The bartender, whom I don't know and isn't wearing a name tag, looks past me toward the door that leads outside.

I feel it the minute she draws attention to it.

Brooks turns first and laughs, slapping his hand on the bar. "Looks like your queen just arrived."

It's hard as hell not to look, but I fight the urge to get another glimpse of her. Over the years, I would google Gillian only to see the one public picture on her private social media. It was never enough, and some years went by with the same picture. Now I only live miles away from her, but it might as well be like I'm back in San Francisco.

"Laurel!" I look over at my cousins and see Romy waving. "Gillian!"

"I guess that seals the deal. We won't be sitting with your cousins tonight." Brooks stares into his plastic beer cup.

"Is something going on with you and Lottie?" I ask, picking up on the fact that Brooks hasn't gone a minute without looking their way and now appears depressed because my ex just joined them.

"What? No."

Melvin diverts all eye contact, definitely giving me the feeling that Brooks has poured his heart out to Melvin at some point.

"That's not very convincing," I say.

"I stop in at the store when I'm on shift to grab a coffee or lunch." He shrugs. "She's always there and acts like I'm inconveniencing her. We're sparking up a friendship."

"I don't think so," the blonde bartender says.

"I'm sorry, we haven't met yet. I'm Ben." I stick out my hand.

"I know." She moves over to help someone else.

"Why do I feel like a stranger in this town?" I grumble.

Brooks slaps me on the shoulder. "There've been some transplants in the last fourteen years." Someone comes over and talks to Melvin, so Brooks slides off the stool. "See ya, Mel."

We wave goodbye, and the guy slides onto the stool Brooks was on.

"What's going on with you?" I ask on our way to an empty picnic table a little too close to the girls.

My eyes can't stop veering in Gillian's direction. She looks way too young and too good to have a freshman in high school. I hate the fact she changed out of her yoga pants and T-shirt into a pair of cutoff jeans and a tighter shirt that's snug across her tits. Her hair isn't pulled back but curled into ringlets, and her face is covered in makeup. She looks hot as hell, and if she knew I was going to be here, it's definitely a "look what you gave up" look. But I still prefer her the way she was at the library.

Brooks clears his throat, pulling my attention back to him.

"Sorry, what's new with you?" I ask.

His eyes divert to the table with my cousins and back to me. "Tipped some cows the other day."

I shake my head. "I'm guessing not at Plain Daisy Ranch since Jude would kick your ass."

"I'm not a fifteen-year-old jackass anymore. Learned that the first time your dad caught me."

I laugh and smack the table. "I remember that. Made you work the farm for a month. And now you're the sheriff."

"And arresting kids for the same shit I used to do." He grins and finishes his beer, standing.

I know he's going to go get another one, but I spot Gillian walking toward the bar. I bolt up out of my seat. "I'll get the next round."

"Just like when I was fifteen, you're following Adams around," he calls after me.

I ignore the jab, but he's got a point. I was definitely more into Gillian than my friends when I was in high school. Sure, we all hung out most of the time, but there were nights I just wanted it to be Gillian and me.

The blonde bartender, whose name I still don't know, eyes me approaching as she talks to Gillian. Obviously, they're friends. She must tell Gillian I'm on my way because Gillian glances over her shoulder and turns her back to me even more.

I'm not going to relent. I want to talk this out. I want to be civil and not feel uncomfortable if we're in the same room.

"Two beers," I tell the blonde, hoping she scurries off and leaves me alone with Gillian.

Instead, she turns to the other bartender and asks him to

get my drinks. I don't know him either, but he barely looks at me while filling the beers and sliding them toward me.

After I pay, I linger, and the tension is like a bubble ready to pop between us. "Gillian," I say, figuring she'll ignore me unless I start the conversation.

She circles around with a sweet, forced fake smile. "Noughton. I didn't see you there."

I grind my teeth at the fact that she's still playing this game of calling me by my last name. "Well, *Adams*, I thought you saw me when you walked in." My gaze falls over her body, appreciating her outfit all the more now that I'm closer.

"Cute. Do the women in San Francisco like your flirty games?"

The blonde hands Gillian a drink. Gillian's glossed lips tempt me as she places them around the tiny straw, sucking the fruity drink up through it.

I shift my stance, and her eyes stray to my crotch. Yeah, she still wants me. She might hate me, but the sexual tension is alive and kicking between us.

"I don't much care about the women in San Francisco."

She rolls her eyes, not believing me. "Excuse me." She abandons her drink and walks inside the bar.

I rush back over to the table and leave the two beers with Brooks before I follow her.

"I'm not sure—"

Whatever he's going to say dies when the door shuts behind me.

I spot Gillian sauntering down the short hallway toward the bathrooms. "Gill—"

She whips around, and her fake smile has been replaced with a pissed-off expression. "You don't get to call me that."

My shoulders fall, and I step closer. "Will you just let me say I'm sorry?"

"Is that all you want?"

"Well... I—" Not even close.

"You don't have to apologize. We weren't the first high school sweethearts who thought they'd make it and didn't. I knew when you went to Clemson that you'd see what life had to offer you outside of Willowbrook and never look back."

"No." I shake my head. "You don't understand."

"I'm sure I don't. Just like you don't understand what it was like here for me. It's great that you're home. I'm sure your family is really happy. But stop trying to talk to me. We don't have anything else to say to each other."

I step forward, and she draws back. I inch a little closer, my hand reaching out and she doesn't move. I want to hug her and hold her and tell her how much I missed her. My arms are open and ready to embrace her. Our eyes lock, and her chest rises and falls. My own heartbeat hammers. Right as my fingers graze her temple, she flinches, turning her head away from me. My hand hangs in the air and I stare down at her, searching for an answer to why for a split second, fear stuck in her eyes, as if she thought I would physically hurt her.

"Gillian."

"Nope." She spins around and barrels into the women's bathroom.

Fucking hell. I lean my back against the wall and bump the back of my head against the hard surface.

What exactly happened while I was away?

Chapter Eight

GILLIAN

I work as a court stenographer all week, but on Saturday afternoons, I help Laurel in the bakery. I handle the front while she's usually preparing some elaborate cake in the back. It's a nice way for me to get my mind off the bar exam. Since Clayton's gotten older, he's really all about his friends.

Plus, I love the people in Willowbrook, and it allows me to chat with the usuals when they come in for their sweet treat.

"So, you didn't tell me what happened last night when you went to the bathroom. I didn't want to ask in front of Lottie and Romy." Laurel ices the wedding cake she's making, her eyes on the details, while I put together a box of cookies and treats destined for The Harvest Depot. Lottie said she'd send someone to come get them this morning to sell at the country store on the Noughton property.

"Do you want the play-by-play? I peed, washed my—"

She stops icing the cake and glares. "You know what I'm talking about."

"What?"

"The bull of a man who followed you inside?"

I stick out my tongue, and she continues icing. Her ability

58

to make it appear like lace is strewn over the cake is what has made her famous in our tri-county area.

I sit on a stool, tape the box, and push it aside, watching her work. If someone comes in, I'll hear the bell. "Same as last time. He tried to talk to me, and I said no."

"You looked a little flushed when you returned to the table."

My head tilts. "It's June, Laurel."

"You know what I mean. This has to be hard for you."

"He'll be gone soon." I cross my fingers under the table because he's being kind of relentless, something I didn't expect. And the fact I've already run into him three times in the first week of his being back shows how small this town is.

"Are you sure about that? I heard Coach Marks is pushing him hard to help out this season. Romy told me last night that Mr. Noughton is making him build his own house on the property. If he starts building that house, I'd take it as a sign that he's staying longer than you think." She switches out the icings and eyes me as if her point wasn't made.

I shrug. "Then it will be me who leaves."

She huffs. She and Clayton are on the same page about us moving. "Stop talking about it."

"I still have to pass the bar, and even if I pass it the first time, I'd have to interview and find a job."

"Why not just start a business here?"

"So Clayton and I can starve?" There's no way Willowbrook would keep me busy enough to make a living. I've scraped by my entire life, and this is my time to finally have what I've always wanted. Financial freedom.

"You're not starving now."

"I will be if I have to live off what I'm making now *and* pay back my school loans."

"I can give you more hours here. I need a delivery person."

I laugh. "I could never handle the stress of getting one of

those to a wedding. With my luck, I'd take a turn too fast and have to tell the bride I ruined her cake."

"You'd be fine, but I get it. I want you to have the world, but I'm going to miss you."

I hug her from behind. She has no idea how much I'll miss her too. "I love you, and I won't be far. Promise."

"No New York?"

"I doubt I'd ever fit in there."

The bell rings at the front of the store, and I squeeze her thin frame one more time before going to the storefront area.

"Welcome to The Sugar Cottage..." My feet skid to a stop on the black-and-white linoleum. "Was I not clear last night?"

Ben holds up his hands and doesn't approach me. "Lottie sent me. The store got slammed because of the new line of goat cheeses, and since I'm the errand boy, here I am."

"I'll be back." I twirl around in my Converses. In the back, Laurel looks at me, and I groan. "He's here."

"Who?"

I cock my hip out to the side. "Really?"

She giggles. "Looks like I should remind you that we do not treat our customers poorly, but in this instance, I'm happy to make an exception."

I grab the box. "Lottie sent him, and she knows I work here on Saturdays."

"I think someone is playing games..."

"I think so too."

"Want a bodyguard?" She places the icing bag down on her tray.

"No, I can handle Ben Noughton."

If only he didn't look so good. Seeing him in the flesh isn't for the faint of heart. He went from a boy with his hat on backward, driving a dirty old pickup truck, to a grown man with wide shoulders and muscles in places I didn't know you could have muscles. Rather than boyish good looks, he's handsome, distinguished, and a little too beautiful, if I'm honest. Although my heart still hurts when I see him, I miss my rugged rancher who wasn't so put together.

"Here you go." I hold out the box, dodging eye contact.

He takes it from me. "I'm not trying to hound you."

I take a quick glance, and as always, his puppy dog eyes kill me. I blow out a breath. "I know. I think someone is arranging these meet-ups."

And I'm going to kill Lottie when I see her next.

His eyes widen as if he just thought about that possibility. "Not unless they have some kind of surveillance on you. I know my family would love for us to get together again, but they're not that stealthy."

"My routine isn't hard. Sure, they'd have to figure out it was my cleaning day for the dentist. But I'm at the library a lot, which could be why Bennett asked you to return Wren's books. Romy messaged Laurel for us to join her last night at the bar. And Lottie knows I work here on Saturdays."

His lips press together. "That is a lot of unlikely coincidences."

"So no, I don't think you're seeking me out." I shuffle my feet and concentrate on the cash register.

"Doesn't mean I don't want to. I really want us to talk, Gillian."

I glance at him. "I'm just..." How can I say I'm not ready? It's been over fourteen years. But I'm not sure I've ever really processed my feelings about what went down between us. I didn't really have the luxury, what with being a young single mother and helping to raise my siblings. "Fine."

"Really?" His brown irises light up. "How about we head to Lincoln?"

"I'd rather stay close."

He bites his cheek. "I don't want to be where people will be staring at us. It's just a reminder."

He has a point, so I relent with another option. "Hickory then."

"I'll take it."

"During the daytime."

"Okay."

"And not a full meal. Coffee?"

"How about breakfast tomorrow? We can go to The Stack, and you can have all the cinnamon rolls you want."

I haven't been there since he left town. It was one of our last meals together before he got in his dad's truck for the airport.

"I'm not sure." There are way too many memories there, but the idea of those cinnamon rolls makes my mouth water. "Fine."

"Great. Do you still live at your dad's house?"

I'm jolted by his question. It feels weird that he doesn't know where I live—someone who used to know everything about me. I didn't even think about it until just now, how far removed he's been from my life. I should've moved on by now, and it's high time I did. I can handle a breakfast with Ben Noughton. And then I can finally move on.

"No. I live on Chesterfield. Eleven ten."

"Great. I'll pick you up." He drops some cash on the counter, picks up the box, and shoots me one of his smiles. The one I'd see in all his endorsements. The one that tugs at my heart.

"Actually, I'll meet you there."

He stops, the door halfway open. Tourists who travel in on the weekends meander on the sidewalk. At least they don't know who he is to me. "Why?"

How can he even ask that question? Because I don't want to sit in the cab of a truck a few feet away from him. I don't want the memories that prick me when they surface to feel too real. "Because we shouldn't be seen together."

It's not the best lie, but there is a sliver of truth there. If we're seen, the rumors will ignite into an inferno.

"I'll handle that."

"But—"

"Please, Gillian. I'm only asking for one breakfast and a twenty-minute drive each way. I know I don't deserve it, and I shouldn't push this, but..." He glances down and lifts his gaze back up to me. "After this, I'll leave you alone. Hell, I'll leave town if you want me to."

He's pulling on my soft side, and damn it, I'm going to let him. But maybe since this could be our last time together, I'll torture myself one more time. "Fine, but don't be late. And if word gets out—"

"It won't."

"Fine."

His smile could light up UNL's Memorial Stadium, and I hate that a piece of me loves that I made him happy. "See you tomorrow."

Ben walks out, and I slump over on the counter.

"Did you really just agree to breakfast? What happened to you calling him Noughton and giving him the cold shoulder?" Laurel laughs as if it were comical that I even tried to resist him.

"Turns out the fourth time seeing him, I can't keep up my front. How will I get through an entire breakfast?"

"Eat fast?"

"Laurel..." I sigh.

"It was inevitable. Have the conversation, get it over with, and move on." She returns to the back.

"I need to borrow that obnoxious sun hat you bought in Jamaica two years ago."

"Then you'll just draw more attention to yourself!" she shouts from the back.

She has a point. Even if I wore my cowgirl hat, I'd have to

take it off when we got inside the restaurant. Maybe Lincoln was the better option, but I don't want to spend that much time with him in the truck.

But Laurel's right. I have to stop dodging him and face this head-on. Surely we've moved on in fourteen years. There's no way that what I still feel for Ben is anything other than the nostalgic remnants of first love. Once we talk and get the past all out on the table, the unrest chaos inside of me will calm.

I hope.

Chapter Nine

BEN

I tiptoe down the stairs Sunday morning, unable to sleep from the excitement of having Gillian to myself today. Trying to disguise myself a bit, I put on my baseball cap and wear my oldest jeans with a T-shirt that's seen better days. Matched with my cowboy boots, the only item in my closet that still fits me, I look like any other rancher in town. It's a lot for her to give me this chance, and I'm not going to put her in harm's way with more nasty gossip or rumors.

I hear the voices before I have time to turn around, my dad spotting me as he stands in the kitchen in front of the open fridge. The door shuts, and I wince.

"Jesus, Dad."

He stands in his boxer briefs, looking unapologetic. I walk into the kitchen and sigh. A blondish woman sits at our kitchen table, wearing my dad's flannel checkered shirt and nothing else.

"Hi." I raise a hand.

She looks at my dad and back at me. "I'm Claudette."

"This is my middle boy, Ben." He sits next to Claudette, handing her a coffee. "Why are you up so early?"

"Um… I could ask you the same thing."

He and Claudette laugh. At least she's his age. I wasn't sure in the years I've been away if they'd gotten younger.

"This is late for me," Dad says. "I'm a cattle rancher. And you're about to be one too. Starting tomorrow, you either work the ranch or find something else to do, but you don't freeload. Enough with being everyone's gopher."

"Freeload? It's my childhood home."

The back door opens, and Emmett flies in, breezes by me, and barrels up the stairs.

"You're on me, but he can come take a shit in his childhood bathroom?" I ask.

"He built his own house." Dad sips his coffee and puts his hand on Claudette's thigh.

I have to get outta here.

"Just because you have a lot of money doesn't change the fact that you're thirty-two years old and should be living on your own."

"I'll pay rent."

"Noughtons aren't lazy."

This conversation is about to get heated. My pulse increases, and I'm not doing that in front of one of his lady friends. Still, I find it hard to bite my tongue. "I got my ass kicked every week and got up to do it all over again. I'm not sure I know any professional football player who's lazy."

"Your dad told me. San Francisco, huh? Very impressive." Claudette smiles.

"Thanks." I squeeze out a forced smile. Where did he find this one that she doesn't know who we are? I'm not buying the charade. Then again, maybe it's her way of changing the subject.

"Regardless, if you don't want to walk into scenes like this, then get your own house. Your property line runs along Emmett's."

"Fine, I'll talk to some contractors this week. Who knew after all the years you wouldn't want me home for a little while."

"No contractors. You do it yourself. You have great hands, and you know enough. If you don't, ask your brothers or cousins."

I gape at him. "I can get out sooner if I hire someone."

With my mom dying so young, my dad took on the role of both parents, but he's never nurtured us. Instead, he believed in making us into self-sufficient men. Which I understand, and I'm sure his dad was the same to him. But I've been here a week. I'm not loafing around.

"That's not the point. Don't you want to sit in your own house and feel accomplished?"

Claudette buries her head in her coffee, and I'm surprised my dad is coming at me so hard with her here. Maybe she's more of a regular than I know.

"I'd feel just as accomplished if I paid someone."

He shakes his head at me. "That's sad. Hate to break it to you, but no strangers on our land. They'll be tearing down trees and ruining our soil with their big trucks and bulldozers."

I shake my head and grab the keys to the old truck. "Nice to meet you, Claudette. See you later."

"Where are you going?" my dad asks.

"Out. I'm thirty-two, remember?"

"One more thing. If you don't want to work the ranch, then I suggest you take up Coach Marks on his offer. You can't forget the little people who helped you get to where you are."

I shake my head, pushing open the screen door and turning to face him. "I'm not meant to be a coach. I have no idea what to do with kids."

"Then you'll be the low man on the ranch. Which means you'll have all the shit jobs. Literally."

I shake my head and hear Claudette say maybe he's being too hard on me, but my dad tells her I've gotten soft with my plush lifestyle in San Francisco.

Funny, since he pushed me into football and forced me to be serious about it since everyone in this town thought I might be something special. There are a lot of people I have to thank for getting me where I am. My dad is one of them. But it took a lot of my own hard work to accomplish what I did, and I don't understand how he can forget all that.

The old family truck that was practically mine in high school sits in the garage, and I have to wonder when the last time it was driven. But I only have to get it to Brooks's house. He said he'd loan me one of his trucks so no one would suspect us in Hickory. When he's not a sheriff, he remodels old trucks. I told him I wanted a junker, though, not one of the shiny ones that would only draw attention.

I turn the key in the engine, and it starts a little rough, but I run the dust off it, winding through the ranch roads, driving through the arches, and out to the country roads. The windows were already rolled down, and I put my arm out, the warm morning air flowing inside the cab as the sun rises over the corn fields in the distance. This, I missed—the kind of solitude I never found in a big city.

It isn't until after I've stopped at Brooks's to switch out the trucks and roll onto Gillian's street, that I grow anxious. Her house is a small ranch with flowers edging her landscaped bushes. It suits her. I wish I could go inside, but she's waiting for me outside already.

I start to pull into her driveway, and she shoos me away, pointing at the street. I've barely stopped when she opens the door and slides down in the seat, tipping her hat further down over her face.

"I feel like when we were younger and you were sneaking out of your dad's house."

"Just go." Her eyes widen.

I press the gas, and the engine sputters. Maybe it wasn't the best idea to take a junker from Brooks.

"Where did you get this?" She stays hunched down through downtown.

No one looks our way.

"Brooks."

"You couldn't get one of the nice ones?"

"Then people would notice." I turn onto the country highway toward Hickory.

"Good thinking."

"Is that a compliment?"

She straightens in the seat, putting on her seat belt. "No, it's an observation." But she bites her lip to stop from smiling.

Damn, I missed that move when we'd joke around and she'd pretend that what I said wasn't funny.

"Where's Clayton?"

She hesitates. Maybe I'm toeing a line she doesn't want me to. Could be a part of her life she doesn't want to share with me.

"He's sleeping in."

"Something I was never able to do." My dad always ran a tight ship. Sunday was his day to relax, but usually we had to do all kinds of chores. It's quiet for a minute, so I say the first thing that comes to mind. "My dad had a visitor this morning."

Gillian chuckles. "Yeah, I won't fill you in on the rumors about your dad over the years."

"Thanks."

"They say he's a big romancer."

"I thought you weren't going to tell me?" I glance at her, and she smirks.

"Changed my mind."

I shake my head, and she leans forward, changing the radio

station. Once she finds a song she likes, she lays her hand on the bench between us. My right hand tightens on the steering wheel. It would be so easy to go back to how it used to be and take her hand.

We arrive in Hickory, and I park the truck in a row of empty spots at the end of the block.

"Um, are you in need of exercise?" Gillian asks.

"You jumped in my truck like you just robbed a bank, and you want me to park right in front of The Stack?"

"You're sharp in the morning. I'm in dire need of coffee."

I chuckle, forgetting how easily she made me laugh.

When I park, she reaches for the handle of the door. I place my hand on her left one, warmth spreading up my arm. Her soft skin makes me ache with the need to touch more of her—to touch all of her.

"Just sit tight. I'll be right back."

"What? What's your plan, Noughton?" She shuts the door and narrows her blue eyes at me.

"Just wait. I promised there would be no rumors, so let me do my thing."

She bites her lip, probably praying I don't see her smile.

I leave her in the truck, walk with my head down the sidewalk, and slide into The Stack. A flood of memories hit me like I was blindsided by a two hundred and fifty pound linebacker. The booth by the window was always ours, and the memory of the first time I took her here, when I was amazed at the amount of cinnamon rolls she could eat, is front and center. It was almost more than me.

An employee comes to the register, and I give her the fake name for my to-go order. She inspects me while pressing buttons on the cash register. I hand her over cash since they don't accept credit cards, and a kid brings me my bag.

"You sure ordered a lot," the woman says.

The kid studies me, and I tip my head down further. Maybe I should've sent Brooks to pick up the meal and meet me somewhere.

I accept the bag and toss a twenty into the tip jar, getting the hell outta there.

I've sneaked around a lot over the years, but never did I feel as desperate for someone not to recognize me. It's one of the rare times I wish I could not be Ben Noughton, wide receiver for the San Francisco Kingsmen. Then again, that's not who I am anymore. Now I'm Ben Noughton, who used to play for the San Francisco Kingsmen. That realization is still hitting me months after I retired.

I climb into the truck, placing the bag of food between us.

"God, it smells so good." She puts her entire head into the bag and inhales. "I've missed you, little ones."

I'm not sure I understood why she had never returned here until I walked into that small diner and was slammed with all the memories. I could almost envision us sitting at that table. The way she'd put her shoes up on my bench while we waited. Our conversations consisted of our dreams for our shared future. While I was out in the world in places that didn't remind me of Gillian or our time together, she was here, where memories of our time together were unending. Of course she wants to push me away. I'd do the same.

"Where are we going?" she asks, putting her seat belt back on.

"Just wait."

"You aren't getting lucky, so you can cut the romance." Her face is etched with seriousness.

"I never thought I was. But we can't be seen together, so that leaves us with few options. That means you're going to be alone with me. Are you okay with that?"

She scoffs. "You don't scare me, Noughton."

"Well, you scare me, Adams."

She looks at me as I pull into traffic. I always did love surprising her.

Chapter Ten

GILLIAN

I t's a real struggle to be in the cab of this pickup with Ben
and not feel a pull toward him. Never mind the fact that
he went to the trouble of borrowing a truck from Brooks,
picked up our breakfast—the size of the bag says he got a ton
of food—and now we're driving somewhere so no one sees us.

When he pulls off the county road, I realize this place is a
little too familiar. It's a spot we found by accident and would
park and make out. It's high up on a hill, looking down at the
rolling hills of Hickory with the sun still rising to its spot high
in the sky. The fields are all covered in wildflowers.

"We should find somewhere else," I say, unable to bear the
thought of being here as he puts his hand on my headrest to
back into a makeshift spot.

"I like this spot."

"I know what you're doing. I'm just not sure why you're
doing it." As soon as the truck stops, I get out, hoping the
fresh air will clear my head.

His truck door opens and shuts, but I don't turn around.
"I'm not sure what you're asking."

I slowly turn while he grabs a blanket, lines the bed of the truck with it, and places the bag of food on it. He pulls out a small cooler with some drinks.

"This isn't a 'let's-clear-the-air-so-we-can-be-friends' setup." I put my hand out, gesturing to everything he's doing. "This is a 'let-me-kiss-you-and-lay-you-down-on-the-truck-bed' arrangement."

He laughs and sits down, patting the spot next to him.

I cross my arms. "I'm not seventeen anymore. Your charm won't work."

"Charm? You thought I had charm in high school?" His expression says he finds that impressive. "I was just horny."

I shake my head. I guess his humor didn't change. "You know what I mean. This elaborate setup. There's no chance of us getting back together."

He takes the food out of the bag, not looking at me. "You'd prefer if I had us sit on the gravel and handed you a takeout container and a plastic fork? You know I wasn't raised like that."

His words ring true. All the Noughton boys have reputations similar to their father's. The women in their lives, the ones they really care about, are treated like queens. You see it with Jude and his best friend, Sadie. They might not be romantically involved, but you'd never guess with how he makes her a plate at the barbecue, gets all her drinks at the bar, and is always the driver when they go anywhere. I think she's the only one he doesn't grunt at.

"So, this is just to be nice?" I tilt my head.

He nods and takes his pointer finger, making a cross over his heart.

"That doesn't hold a lot of weight."

He pats the spot next to him. "They're going to get cold."

I forgot about the cinnamon rolls, but I don't want to give in too soon. He'll see me as weak when I'm adamant that nothing is happening between us.

Still, I slide up onto the truck bed where he has an entire spread of breakfast items. One container is filled with little cinnamon rolls. How I managed to not have these in all the years he's been away makes me think I have more willpower than I give myself credit for.

He stabs one with a fork and holds it out to me.

"I can get it myself." I pick up my own fork and put one on my plate. I pile part of a cheese omelet and some fruit there too.

The moan that escapes him after he takes his first bite zeros in between my thighs. "I forgot how good they were. How good most of the food is around here."

"You have to have good food in San Francisco." I bite into a piece of melon.

"Had," he says.

"Excuse me?"

"I'm not going back to San Francisco, so I *had* good food there." There's something on his face that I can't read.

"Does that mean you're staying in Willowbrook?"

He shrugs. "I'm not sure. My dad asked me to come home, so here I am. But now he wants me to work the ranch or go help Coach Marks. And he wants me out of my childhood bedroom and is forcing me to build my own house. I don't know. Maybe it was always the assumption I would return when my career was done."

I hate that my heart is tugging for him. Leaving Willowbrook wasn't an easy decision for him. Everyone knows that although Jude is proud, he's somewhat resentful he had to stay and take over the ranch because ranches stay in the family around here and he's the oldest brother. I wonder how he'd feel if Ben started on the ranch, too, after he's built it up to what it is today.

"Is that what you want?"

He shrugs again, piling more food into his mouth.

"You're old enough to make your own decisions."

Maybe I'm lucky that I lost my mom young, my dad worked himself to death, and my siblings moved away. I have no family to have any expectations of me. But it's hard at times. Feeling alone. Sure, I have Clayton and Laurel and the people in town, but one thing I loved about being with Ben was feeling like a part of the Noughton family. Something I never really had growing up. They were all very kind to me. I still get invited to parties today, but it's not the same. Eventually, Ben will marry someone else, and she's not going to want his high school sweetheart lingering around.

"I don't really wanna talk about it," he says.

"Then what do you want to talk about?" I grab another cinnamon roll because I'll probably never go back. They wouldn't be the same without Ben.

"How we can get back to being friends."

I shake my head and shove a roll into my mouth so I have the excuse of chewing.

He waits patiently, eating his food and opening the orange juice he brought with him.

When I swallow, I sigh. "I'm going to be honest. I'm not sure there's a possibility of that. I mean. Us. Friends?"

"You were my friend first."

"Yeah, but then we were so much more." Our eyes lock and hold for a beat, until I strip my gaze away.

"I'm sorry for what happened."

I leave my plate and slide off the truck bed, wrapping my arms around myself and watching the sun shine over the fields.

"I'm not sure what else I can say." His voice is low.

I hear him getting off the truck too. "It's not that. What happened isn't so bad that I don't forgive you. Looking back, I was probably pretty needy."

"No. You weren't. Please don't think that."

I turn to him, and he grabs my hands. A zing of electricity

bolts through my body. I assumed that his hands would be soft as if he got manicures every week, but they're still rough with the calluses I remember.

"Leaving Willowbrook was hard. When I got to school, there were so many expectations of me. I didn't know anyone. I was lost, so fucking lost. And I handled it like shit—"

My chest gets tight, and I realize that maybe rehashing the past wasn't such a good idea. "Please stop. I don't want to talk about it. I don't want to go back there."

Mostly because of my own actions. After such a short time, I slept with someone else because I was lonely and ended up pregnant, ensuring the two of us would never get back together.

"I love Clayton, and I'll never regret that I got pregnant. I can't apologize for that."

"I would never ask you to."

I strip my hands out of his. His touch is too tempting and makes me want to crawl into his arms and make the pain go away. "Good."

"Come back and eat. We can have a lighter conversation. It doesn't have to be so heavy. We can save that for another time." He grabs my hand and tugs me gently to follow him.

"I'm not sure there's going to be another time. You don't know if you're staying, and I'm taking the bar exam soon. If I pass, I'm looking for a new job... outside of Willowbrook."

He drops my hand. "Oh."

"We can circle one another for a little bit and be fine. If we were both planning on staying here, I'd say let's hash it out, but one or both of us are leaving."

Hurt lines his eyes, and I'm not sure why, since he said himself that he might not be sticking around.

"You went to law school?" he asks.

"No one told you?" Here I thought his family was feeding him information about me over the years.

He shrugs. "All I've ever done is stalk your socials, and you're piss poor at updating them."

I laugh. "You're kidding, right? Lottie? Romy? Emmett? No one told you anything?" One time I had no one to call when my car broke down, and Emmett came to my rescue.

"I'm not very receptive when your name comes up. They tried to tell me things at first, but I'd change the subject. It hurt that you were moving on without me."

"Is that so?" I roll my eyes.

"Just because I was the one who left, doesn't mean it didn't hurt. I'd never felt more alone in my life. And it took me a long time to get used to not being in Willowbrook with you and my family and friends."

I've never really thought about his side of things. I assumed Clemson was all fun and games for him. He was off living his dream while my life had stalled.

"So, you got to ignore my life while I had to hear about you all the time, watch you on television, see you in ads in magazines. I'd be going about my life, having a pretty good day, taking Clayton to the doctor, picking up a magazine, and bam, there you were. Don't get me started on the Google searches I did when you weren't single."

He leans against the open truck bed, arms crossed. "You can't believe all the pictures you see."

"So you weren't on dates?"

"Are you suggesting that you haven't dated the entire time I've been gone?" He raises his eyebrows.

"It's not easy when you're a single mom. Briar would watch Clayton sometimes, but I never wanted to date. I just wanted adult conversation, and Laurel handled that."

"So, there've been no other guys?" His eyebrows haven't come down, and I can see he's not going to let this go.

"Only a few. Not nearly the amount you've had, and none of mine were models."

His hands move to grip the edge of the bed, and his knuckles whiten. After a beat, he circles around and leans over the bed of the truck to grab both of our coffees.

I admire his ass in his worn jeans. Why does he have to be so damn good-looking? Why can't he have gotten uglier over the years? Maybe have grown moles all over his face? Or his teeth turned yellow from not going to the dentist?

Ben clears his throat, and I look up from his crotch.

"I wasn't..." I feel my cheeks heat.

A sexy, flirty smirk crosses his face. One I'm sure earned him a lot of attention from the women who wanted to bed a pro player. "It's okay. I always loved your eyes on me."

"You need to stop." I take my coffee from his hands, and our fingers brush. The coffee slips from my grasp, splattering over the gravel ground and on my shoes "Shit."

Ben laughs, holding his coffee out to me.

I shake my head. "It's not funny."

He slowly stops laughing, his face growing more serious. "What? The fact that you still want me as bad as you did when you were a seventeen-year-old?"

I stare blankly at him. "No."

"It's okay. I want you as much as a thirteen-year-old boy who just saw his first set of tits."

I point at him. "See, you can't talk to me like that."

He shrugs. "I'm being truthful."

"You're causing trouble, Noughton."

"You should know, I'm starting to get off on you calling me Noughton."

My fists clench, my patience running on its last drop. "Then I'll have to find something else to call you."

"Can't wait to see what you come up with." He flashes me a smile.

Both of our phones go off at the same time, and I scurry to the truck bed to dig into my sweatshirt, hoping it's not anything to do with Clayton. Then again, why would both of our phones go off?

We each answer the call. I'm not sure who called him, but Laurel is on my other end.

"Coach Marks?" I whisper.

BEN

Gillian packs everything, I grab the blanket, and we're in the cab no more than two minutes after we both received phone calls telling us that Coach Marks suffered a heart attack last night. Laurel called her, and Jude called me.

"I can't believe it. I just saw him yesterday." I turn the key in the ignition and speed away, putting on my seat belt while I drive.

"Did Jude say how he was? Laurel didn't know much."

I shake my head. "He just said that he was headed up there with Dad. No one knows anything yet."

"I better call Clayton. I don't want him to hear it from someone else." She grabs her phone from her pocket. She dials, and she grunts after a few seconds. "Why do I get him a phone if he's not going to answer it?"

I'm sure between our conversation and hearing the news about Coach Marks, she's wound tighter than normal, but it's odd hearing her parental voice.

She presses her screen again and lifts it to her ear, her fingers tapping on her leg.

"We can go there first. Pick him up," I say.

Her thumbs move across the screen, and from the corner of my eye, I see her sending text after text.

"No, I should drive him. Drop me off, and I'll take Clayton up there."

She wipes her face, and I take a quick glance away from the road to see a few tears falling down her cheeks.

"I'm sure he's going to be okay." I touch her knee.

She doesn't pull away, and I want to keep my hand there, but I don't want to overstep. I squeeze and return my hand to the wheel.

"He's done so much for us over the years." She doesn't say anything else, and I have so many questions I want to ask, but now isn't the time. "He's like a second father. Had us over for Christmas last year."

She should have been at my family's house on Christmas. And I should have been the one to invite her.

"I had no idea." Coach Marks was always friendly with Gillian, but I thought it was because she was my girlfriend. Plus, everyone loves Gillian. She's too sweet for anyone to hate.

"You wouldn't." She shakes her head. "Sorry, I didn't mean that. Not how it sounded at least."

"Don't be sorry. I deserve it."

Her phone rings, and I'm happy for the distraction.

"Clay!" Her mom voice is a scary one. "I called you how many times and texted."

He must be saying something because she's silent for a moment.

"Sleeping? Fine. Listen," she says in a more nurturing voice. "Remember, I went out to breakfast." I can hear him on the other end. "A friend." Another pause. "No, not Laurel." She fidgets, straightening her back and cracking her neck. "I'm coming home now, but I have something to tell you."

She wipes her tears with her palm. I wish I could take the phone and tell Clayton myself so she doesn't have to, but at the parade, it was clear the kid doesn't like me. Instead of doing what I want to do, I put my hand on her knee again, this time not letting go. She needs to know I'm here for her right now.

She looks at me, but I ignore her eyes piercing into the side of my head. If she wants my hand off, she can remove it.

"Coach Marks suffered a heart attack last night. As far as I know, he's not in any type of crisis. But I'm on my way home, and we can head up there. Be there in, like, ten?" She poses it as more of a question, her eyes still watching me.

I nod to confirm.

"Just shower quickly and get dressed." She hangs up and stares out the window.

"I'd like to drive you and Clayton to the hospital."

"Thanks, but no."

"Gill..."

She whips her head in my direction and glares at me. We're not at that point yet. Noted.

"Gillian, you aren't in any condition to drive. I'll take you, and you can get a ride home. Hell, I'll give you the truck to drive home if you want."

It takes a minute before she answers, "fine." She leans her head back against the headrest allowing the wind to whip her hair around.

We pull up to her house, and it's like déjà vu, except it's not Gillian waiting for me, but Clayton on the porch, his head buried in his phone. I honk my horn and he lifts his head, rearing back for a moment.

He walks toward Gillian's car, a reliable grayish sedan.

"Clay, come on. Ben's taking us," she calls.

I'm surprised, since it's the first time she's used my name in front of me.

"What? Why?" He glares at us.

"Just come on." She waves.

Clayton lumbers over, his face growing more and more pissed off with every step. Gillian opens the door and slides over next to me. Again, I have to tighten my hand on the steering wheel so I don't put my arm around her. Who knew a habit from over a decade ago was still alive and kicking inside me?

"Hey, Clayton," I say, waiting for him to put his seat belt on.

Gillian elbows him when he doesn't say anything back, and he murmurs, "Hey."

The truck putters for a second, but when I give it more gas, it runs smoother.

"Aren't you worth millions?" Clayton asks. "What's with the rust bucket?"

"Clay!" I do kind of love Gillian's mom voice.

"It's fine." My hand falls to touch her leg, but she slides it away. Glancing to the side, I can see that Clayton clocked the move and his lips thin into a straight line. "I borrowed it from a friend."

"It's Sheriff Watson's," Gillian says.

"Why didn't he give you one of the new ones he fixes up?"

At least the kid is making conversation instead of sulking. "I didn't want one of those."

"Clayton wants one when he turns sixteen." Gillian wraps her arm around her son. "Don't you?"

"I don't know anymore." He shrugs off her touch and, like his mom moments ago, stares out the window. I guess that's the end of our conversation.

For the rest of the ride to the hospital, it's only the warm breeze through the windows and a country station as background noise.

THERE ARE SO MANY CARS AND TRUCKS IN THE hospital parking lot that people have had to find spots on the street. It shows how much Coach Marks is loved in this community. How he's a staple, and if something bad happens, how much they'll mourn. I'm not sure what that would mean for the football season that Willowbrook lives and dies by. Or at least they used to.

I drop off Gillian and Clayton at the emergency door and park the truck.

When I walk in, my dad and Jude are waiting for me as if they knew I'd dropped Gillian off to be a nice guy but also to keep our names out of people's mouths.

"What's the word?" I ask.

Jude shrugs. "They might be transporting him for surgery. Right now, he's stable."

"That's good."

"Maggie is pretty distraught. She's in the waiting room," my dad says.

I peek into the large room, and sure enough, Gillian has her arm around Maggie Marks. Clayton is with a few other kids from the football team, each of them staring at their phones.

A nurse comes out, and everyone stands, thinking we're getting an update. She looks at a small piece of paper in her hand. "Is Ben Noughton here?" She scans the room and locks eyes on me. "Mr. Marks would like to see you."

"Me?"

Maggie wipes the tissue she's holding under her eyes and nods at me, forcing a smile.

"Is there another Ben Noughton here?" Jude shakes his head. "That college degree didn't really do much, huh?"

"Go to hell," I snipe.

I've grown used to Jude's digs, and I usually let them slide off my back. He was left with a lot of responsibility when I jetted off to pursue a dream. Even now, when I offer money, he and my dad act insulted. It's my way of paying them back for allowing me to have the life I've had, but all Jude sees is me showing off.

"This isn't the time, boys." Dad grips my shoulder and stares into my eyes, silently telling me to get my ass over to the nurse.

The nurse scans her pass, and the doors open. Following her, I know what Coach is about to ask me. And I have no idea what my answer will be. I have no idea how to coach or even how to be around teenagers.

I walk into the room, and Coach Marks is sitting up in the hospital bed, a million wires hooked up to him. It's hard to see a man you idolize looking so weak.

"Benny boy!" He eyes the chair next to him.

"Shouldn't you be resting?"

"I'll rest when I'm dead. Sit."

I fold myself into the chair next to his bed, my eyes veering to the monitor with his blood pressure and other numbers.

"I'm going to be hung up for a while. Surgery and then rehab."

"But you'll be fine."

He does the cross over his chest thing and kisses the Saint Christopher medallion around his neck, glancing at the ceiling. "So they say."

"Good." I relax into the chair.

"I can't coach this year. The doc says the stress of it while I'm recovering from bypass and rehab won't allow for it."

"Surely Coach Greer can take over the team."

Greer is the assistant coach, and sure, he might tip the bottle a little too much, but he always shows up for practices and games regardless of his condition.

Coach Marks stares at me unwaveringly. He's not the type of man who ever speaks ill of anyone, especially a man who has stood by his side when Willowbrook wasn't playing great. But he's obviously not comfortable with Greer as the head coach.

"I'm not a coach. I don't even know what to do," I say.

"Bullshit. You're more qualified than me."

I laugh at the absurdity of his words. "No one can fill your shoes."

His cheeks flush. "Thanks for the kind words, Benny, but you can fill them. Now, I don't want to guilt-trip you into it, but I did help get you into the league." His face widens into an ear-to-ear grin. "It would be a nice way for you to pay me back."

I've seen firsthand the way this town can turn if the Wildcats play badly, and I don't want the scrutiny. But how do I tell this man, whom I do feel I owe so much, no? Especially since nothing else has panned out so far. My agent said the analyst job isn't looking great right now. And I am sick of being the errand boy for my family—except for the part where they put me in line with Gillian.

Gillian.

If I stay in Willowbrook a little longer, it gives me time with her. I'm not sure what I want to happen between us. I want her to forgive me, and I want her friendship again, but deep down, I know I want more. It's a hard pill to swallow that I might not get that chance again. That I fucked it up all those years ago, and there's no coming back from it. Sure, she made her decisions after we broke up, but if I'd never screwed it up with her in the first place, things would be so different now. It's complicated as hell, but she's the number one reason to stay in Willowbrook.

"Okay," I say, Gillian's face front and center in my mind. "I'll do it, but only until you're well enough to come back. And I expect hourly phone calls so you can tell me what the hell to do."

His stomach jiggles with his laughter, and he puts out his big, meaty hand. "Thanks, Benny, I owe you one."

I slide my hand into his, standing to my feet. "I'm just paying you back. But you better get better."

"I knew all those naysayers who said you'd abandoned us were wrong. You'll always be a Willowbrook Wildcat." He pats my chest over my heart.

I blink, his words soaking in. *Everyone in this town felt abandoned.*

I don't say anything, and he hits the call button, asking for a pad of paper and a pen. For the next hour, he draws up plays and tells me exactly how to conduct the camps coming up next week.

Chapter Twelve

GILLIAN

Coach Marks was transported to Lincoln for bypass surgery, which apparently went well. He's been healing at home before he starts his cardiac rehab. It's left Ben busy, which has been great because that means he hasn't had time to bother me. I've only run into him once, and that was when I was at The Harvest Depot on the ranch, so I can't exactly blame him for stalking me.

I'd say we can coexist in this town, except for the fact that every time I see a Plain Daisy Ranch truck, I do a double take to see if it's Ben. The disappointment that follows isn't a good sign.

Now I sit in a stiff plastic chair in the high school cafeteria. I loathe the booster club. It's not really a choice when you live in a small town like ours. The majority of people want to help out our athletes and if your kid plays a sport, whether they've reached high school yet or not, you're a member of the booster club. I've been fortunate that they gave me a pass since I was in law school so, I haven't had to organize any tasks. Not that they gave me any slack on my time working the concession stands.

"Let's begin the meeting," Alondra announces, standing at the small podium with a microphone.

I glance around the barely-filled cafeteria. Not sure why we need a microphone, but that's Alondra. She's mom of the year. The one who knows everything that's going on. The one who packs her kids a nutritious lunch with those cute containers that separate their sandwich from their third serving of fruit for the day. She probably wakes up early and makes a full breakfast since it's the most important meal of the day. But it's good that she's in charge. Women like her are who booster clubs were built to be run by. If I were in charge, our players would probably be in ten-year-old uniforms with rips and insufferable smells.

"We've all heard the news about Coach Marks." She lowers her head as if she's saying a quick prayer. When her head perks up, her usual Stepford wife smile is in place. Rarely have I seen a genuinely happy grin on Alondra. "Thankfully, Ben Noughton has agreed to take over the team."

Everyone claps. Feeling eyes on me, I clap as well, though with less enthusiasm than everyone else.

"I know, right? Grayson is so excited to be coached by such a big name in football."

If I didn't have to worry about someone seeing me, I'd stick my finger down my throat and gag.

Alondra looks over the crowd of women and a sprinkle of men, then toward the door, her smile growing with every second. Everyone turns and follows her line of sight.

"And I asked him to come and speak to us today." She holds out her hand, and everyone claps as if the President of the United States is about to give the State of the Union address.

What is going on right now?

Ben walks down the aisle between the chairs, some of the men holding their hands out for high fives. This is ridiculous.

He steps up to the stage, and Alondra opens her arms. Ben's eyes widen, and I bite my lip to prevent myself from laughing at how uncomfortable he looks. He's not the touchy-feely type until you get to know him. When we first started dating, he barely held my hand, but that died quickly. Just the other week, he was trying to hold my leg while we were driving. Just the thought of his big hands on me brings back the rush of goose bumps that climbed my spine that day.

Alondra clings to him and he pats her back, removing himself from their embrace.

Stepping up to the podium, Ben scans the crowd, and small wrinkles crinkle around his eyes when he spots me. The women in front of me turn around to look at me. I give them a small wave.

"Thank you all for having me. I'm gonna be honest, I don't know much about the booster club. Alondra met with me this afternoon and told me all that you've accomplished since she's been president, and it's impressive."

They met this afternoon? The pang of jealousy shouldn't be there, but Alondra was a senior when we were sophomores, and even back then, she always asked him for private interviews for the school newspaper. Did a huge spread on him for the yearbook. She's been crushing on Ben since then, and if the rumors are true, she and Ned are on the brink of divorce. I hope she isn't looking for Ben to replace him.

I shake my head because that's none of my business. Surprisingly, I found some peace that Sunday when I talked to Ben. Sure, we didn't talk it all out, but do we need to? There's no future between us. Once I take the bar exam, I'll have six to seven weeks before I get my results, and I'm not sure what I'll do with my downtime.

Alondra leans forward and grabs the bottom of the silver cord that holds the microphone to the podium. "Go Wildcats!" Ben forces a smile, and she pushes the microphone back to him. "Please carry on."

"Thanks. Taking inventory this past week, I'd really like to get the boys some new gear. The weight room needs more machines. This all costs money of course, which, according to Alondra, is where you guys come in. I'm happy to pitch in where necessary. Obviously, the boys need to be part of the fundraising efforts, so they appreciate the new equipment. But I'm a novice when it comes to all this, so point me in the right direction and tell me where to go."

Alondra's laugh echoes into every nook and cranny in the room.

"Thanks for having me today, and thank you for spending your time helping the student athletes of Willowbrook High." He steps back from the mic, signaling to Alondra that it's all hers.

"Thank you, Coach." She looks over her shoulder at him. "This is an exciting day for Willowbrook."

I sigh, and Drew's mom, who is next to me, elbows me in the ribs. I touch the spot, and Betsy looks around with wide eyes. I guess I did that too loudly.

"I'll elect myself to be in charge of the fundraiser for the football team." Alondra raises her hand. Surprise. Surprise. "This way I can assure that we put our best foot forward."

I lean over to Betsy. "The rest of us are incompetent then?"

"Did you have something to say, Gillian?" Alondra calls me out.

Ben smirks like he used to when I got caught talking in physics.

"Nope. Sounds like a plan. No one better than you to lead the charge." There's sarcasm in my tone, and her smile falters for a second before she smacks her practiced one back in place.

"Well, thank you. That's very kind of you." Her voice is cold.

"Actually." Tori, the vice president, stands with her arm raised.

"Yes, Tori," Alondra says.

"You have so much on your plate. You're in charge of soccer already for your younger kids, so you shouldn't be responsible for football too."

Alondra's eyes glare daggers at Tori, whom I thought was her best friend. Maybe they had a falling out.

I thought it was clear to everyone why Alondra wants to be in charge of football fundraising. Ben.

"It's fine," Alondra says, keeping her smile in place.

"I think Gillian should do it. She's had a pass for a while with law school, but you take the bar next week, right?" Tori turns to me, as does everyone else.

Betsy coughs out a laugh, pretending to have a coughing fit.

"Um... yeah." How does Tori know when I'm taking the bar? I could have very well waited.

"Great. Then you'll have the time," Tori says.

"Um..."

"It's okay, Gillian probably wants to take some time to decompress. Not to mention, very few people pass the bar the first time they take it." Alondra must notice the look on my face. "I'm not saying you won't. It's just facts." She shrugs and smiles as if she means no insult.

"Actually, you're wrong. The majority do pass the first time." Over seventy percent, to be exact. Now that she's insulted me in front of everyone, the side of me that I'm not too proud of comes out. "And I can take on the football fundraiser. No problem."

"Oh, well..." She looks at Ben with a cringe. Does she

93

think he'll have a problem with it? "With your history, I'm not sure..."

"I'm sure they can be adults," Betsy shouts, and I elbow her this time.

"I mean, if Ben would rather not work with me, I'll gladly retract my offer," Alondra says with a bit of a huff.

I'm playing a game. I know I am, because Ben will pick me over Alondra, and I'm slightly ashamed of my behavior. Slightly.

Ben grabs the bottom of the microphone and turns it toward him, staring at me. "I'm good with Gillian." His million-dollar smile lands on me, and my heart pinches in my chest.

Alondra yanks the microphone back to her, and Ben releases it. "Okay then. Gillian is in charge. If it all becomes too much, you'll let me know?"

I stare blankly at her and don't answer.

"That's enough for tonight," she says.

"What about the girls' cross country?" another parent shouts.

Alondra appears flustered, looking through her notecards as if she's lost track of where this meeting was supposed to go. Her ability to go with the flow is nonexistent.

"We'll get to that at the next meeting. Good night, every-one." She takes her notecards and heads to the chair behind the podium that has her messenger bag on it.

"Go Wildcats!" Betsy shouts when Alondra doesn't end the meeting like she always does.

I bite down my laugh until we get into the hallway.

"Tori better watch her back," Betsy whispers as we walk down the hallway.

"Why would she push for me to do it? What did I ever do to her?" I thought Tori liked me, but now I'm not so sure. Calling me out like that in front of everyone as a slacker.

"Whatever her reason, it didn't take you long to agree." Her eyebrows rise.

"Alondra insulted me."

"She insults everyone. I think maybe it's something more?" Betsy looks behind us. "And here he comes."

"What?"

"Hey, ladies," Ben says, walking alongside us. "These booster meetings are pretty entertaining. I might become a regular."

"You mean you're not used to two women fighting over you?" Betsy asks.

I elbow her. It's a surprise we aren't both nursing bruised ribs after these meetings.

Ben stretches his arm in front of me, never losing his stride. "Ben Noughton."

Betsy giggles as she shakes his hand. "I know. I'm Betsy."

"Ben, Betsy moved here after you left. She's Drew's mom, Clayton's best friend."

"Nice to meet you. Drew is very enthusiastic. Great kid."

I'm not sure how much Ben has really been around the boys or if he's only going to coach varsity. Since Clayton and Drew are freshmen they'll be on the junior varsity team.

"Have you seen your shrine?" Betsy signals to the Ben Noughton glass case.

He stops. "Holy shit." Stepping forward, he inspects it further. "Is that my athletic tape?"

"Sure is," Betsy says. "Well, it was nice to meet you, Ben. I have to go and get the little ones to bed."

"I'll walk out with you," I say, ready to say goodbye to Ben.

Betsy hems and haws, staring at Ben. "Oh. I figured you two needed to talk about fundraiser ideas."

I communicate with my eyes to Betsy that I know the game she's playing and I do not appreciate it.

"I didn't eat dinner. Want to go grab a pizza and shoot around some ideas?" Ben asks.

I don't answer.

Betsy swarms me in a hug. "That's a great idea. Clayton's at our house, and Sam fed him already. See you two later." She dislodges from me, and I feel as if I just got off the Tilt-A-Whirl ride.

"You were my ride," I say to her.

She smiles overly big. "I'm sure Ben can get you home. Right, Ben?"

"Definitely."

"Great. Glad it all worked out. See you later." She walks out, falling in line with another parent.

"So?" I ask with a sigh.

"Let's go." He looks at the glass case one more time and turns back to me.

I've seen the case a million times but have never taken the time to truly look at everything. Why I had to be a part of the shrine with our prom king and queen picture, along with other pictures of him while he attended Willowbrook High, I'll never understand.

He places his hand on the small of my back, and his touch lingers longer than it should as we walk toward the doors. The worst part is I don't strip his hand off me when I know I should.

Chapter Thirteen

BEN

The parking lot light shines down on my old truck, and Gillian stops two parking spots away. It's the same one I used to pick her up in. We've made love in the bed more times than I can count.

"I didn't know that your family still had it." She steps forward slowly as if she's approaching a predator.

"My dad had it in the garage on the property. I had Sarge do what he had to so it would run again."

She looks shocked, as if she thought my money would mean I'd just replace the things that meant the most to me. This truck holds a lot of memories. The majority of them are with her, but also Jude and I squeezing Emmett between us until he'd get so annoyed he'd start swinging. My dad driving us to my mom's gravesite on her birthday, with shovels and rakes and flowers piled in the back so everyone knew how much she was loved and missed.

I open the door for her. She used to always kiss me and give me a flirtatious smirk before climbing in. This time, she just props herself up on the beat-up vinyl seat and crosses her legs, staring at me to shut the door.

I blink, losing myself down memory lane again.

I round the truck and purposely don't acknowledge the booster club people pretending not to watch us.

"You cool with being seen with me this time?" I'm not trying to sound like an ass. I honestly want to know.

"Now that it's been announced to everyone that I'm in charge of the fundraisers, it's fine."

"Great. Cheeseburger pizza from By the Slice?"

"You can strip the 'I know what you love' look from your face, but yeah."

I laugh and start the truck, happy that her food preferences haven't changed. "Good. I haven't had it since I've been back." I put my hand on the back of her headrest and back out of the spot.

"Really? You used to love the cheeseburger pizza."

I pause, second-guessing what I want to say, but at this point, fuck it. "I didn't want to eat there without you."

"What?"

I stop at the light and face her. Her forehead crinkles.

The light turns green, and I accelerate, giving myself time to come up with the right response. "I thought maybe I only enjoyed it so much because I liked being there with you. Watching how much you enjoyed it."

"Oh." She tucks one hand between her crossed legs.

I really need her to stop doing things to draw attention to her bare legs.

"Does that mean you're going to watch me like some creep while I eat?"

I shake my head, thankful she turned it into a joke. We made some progress a few weeks ago before we got the news about Coach Marks, but we're still in this awkward stage where we're not friends yet. "Would that bother you?"

"Yes, very much."

I glance over, and she's smiling. That has to mean progress.

I pull into the parking lot of By the Slice, and since it's a little later, it's not packed full of families. I turn off the engine and climb out of the cab. Sadly, Gillian does the same, so I'm not able to open the door for her.

She meets me at the back of the truck, her purse crossways over her body, resting between her tits. I'm left adjusting myself as slyly as I can on the way into the restaurant. Beating off in the shower isn't taking off the edge anymore.

She talks to the hostess, and this isn't the first time I'm surprised about someone she knows that I don't. So many new people have come to Willowbrook or the surrounding towns since I moved away, which I guess is to be expected. But when I was in San Francisco and pictured back home, I always imagined it to be exactly how I left it.

The young hostess sits us at a table smack dab in the middle of the place. Might as well put a spotlight on us too.

"This is awkward," I say, lifting my menu.

"Thank goodness it's not Saturday night." She tips her menu down, smiling at me.

"We'd definitely be on the Canary Wall again."

"I paid Tammy to take that down," she says and puts her finger over her lips.

"How did you manage that? And she got past Melvin?"

She puts her menu on the table, leaning over, and her tits distract me for a second. By the time my eyes reach hers, she's clocked that I was staring at her chest. She doesn't say anything, but the flush on her cheeks makes me think I'm not the only one feeling the sexual tension.

"Melvin loves Tammy. Like, loves her and will pretty much do anything she asks."

"But that goes against the entire code of the Canary Wall."

"Are you really arguing the ethics of the Canary Wall?"

"No. I'm just saying she's messing with the rules. I'm assuming Tammy is the blonde bartender?"

She nods. "She's new to town too. It seems like she's been around for a long time, though. She's good people."

"She wouldn't give me the time of day."

"She's Team Adams." She leans back and opens her menu again.

My fingertips tip her menu down, and Gillian wears a sheepish smile.

"Team Adams?" I ask.

She nods. "Some people took sides when you left. I may have recruited Tammy after a night at The Hidden Cave when I had a smidge too much to drink." She opens a small space between her finger and thumb.

"Do I even want to ask how many people were Team Noughton?"

She lowers her menu all the way to say something, but the server interrupts to take our order.

"Do you mind?" I ask Gillian, and she shakes her head. I look at the server, a boy who reminds me a lot of me when I was young. "An extra-large cheeseburger pizza with extra cheese and two salads. Italian on one and ranch?" My eyes go to Gillian, and she nods. "Ranch on the other."

"You got it, Coach Noughton." He walks away, and I watch him as he goes.

"Is he a football player?" I thumb in the kid's direction.

Gillian laughs. "No, but Coach Marks was Coach Marks to a lot of kids who never played. Welcome to your new role in Willowbrook, Coach Noughton."

It's weird, but it warms my chest at the same time. Maybe because I always respected Coach Marks so much.

"You must be starving," she says.

"Yes, and this could be the last time I ever eat cheeseburger pizza."

She shakes her head, but there's amusement in her expression. "Why would that be?" She knows why, but I kind of like her playing clueless—it gives me a chance to woo her.

"Same reason I haven't been here since I got back to town. It's not the same unless I eat it with you."

"Good line, Noughton."

"I'm serious. I never got over you."

She rolls her eyes. I hope one day I can convince her how much of my heart she kept when I stepped on that plane to Clemson.

"What's your game plan here?" She tilts her head, studying me.

"What do you want it to be?"

She shakes her head, thanking the server for bringing us some water. She taps the end of the straw on the table to free it from the wrapper. "You're not throwing it back to me. I'm serious. We're going to be working on a few things together now. Are we supposed to be friends?"

I do the same with my straw and blow my wrapper at her. She swats it away and laughs. I missed that sound more than I ever admitted to myself.

"I thought I could, but I've realized I can never just be your friend. I mean, if I had to. If you were with someone, maybe I'd force—yeah, no. I can't be your friend, Gillian." I meet her blue gaze, hoping she'll see the truth of my words.

She props her elbows on the table and leans forward. "You're not even staying in town."

"I'm here for the season. It's going to take time for Coach Marks to get better, so I'm not going anywhere for a while."

She leans back in her chair, fiddling with her fingers. "Well, I'm taking the bar exam next week and should have the results in six or seven weeks. Assuming I pass, I'll be interviewing after that and am not sure where I'll end up."

My stomach sours at the thought of her leaving, which is

stupid because I don't even know where the hell I'll end up. I try not to let it show. "It's impressive what you were able to accomplish with Clayton."

"Well, thanks, but you're changing the subject. I haven't forgotten my original question. What do you want?"

"I'm not sure I understand the question. We're here to discuss fundraising, right?"

She studies me for a beat. "I'm not into games, Noughton."

I look around and lean over the table, lowering my voice. "You want the truth? Here it is. I never fell out of love with you. I was an asshole to leave things how they were between us. I can't sit across from you and tell you that I want to have a coach-slash-booster mom relationship with you. Nor do I want a friendship. I want you in my bed, Gillian. I want to kiss you when I want. I want to hold your hand when we walk into a room. I want everyone to know that you're mine. But I know we don't know where our futures are going, and they might go in different directions again. So I'm not sure how to solve this problem. Which means that even though I know what I want, I'm not sure I can have it."

She blows out a breath and stares around the room that's growing less crowded by the minute. Her eyes well with tears.

My stomach plummets to my feet. "Fuck, I didn't mean to make you cry."

She shoos me with her hand, sucking back the tears before they fall. "I waited so long to hear those words. I always thought you just forgot me."

"Never." It takes all my willpower not to get out of my chair and fall to my knees in front of her. "I could never forget you, Gillian. You're the love of my life."

A strangled sound comes out of her. "I'm not sure... I mean... I don't know. I can't get attached to you just to get my heart broken again."

"What if we take it slow? I know I said I couldn't be your friend, but I can try. I'll do anything if there's hope for more."

Her gaze darts toward the door, and I'm afraid she's going to run out of here.

"I'm not sure."

Our pizza arrives, and the server puts it on the metal tray and hands us two plates. I guess we're not getting our salads, but that's okay because the pizza looks way too good.

I lift a slice, and she raises her plate.

"Will you think about it?" I ask.

"Friends?" she asks with a wince. She doesn't like that word to describe us either. Good.

"If that's where we have to start."

"And what happens if it grows to more? What happens if feelings surface again?"

"Are you suggesting that you lost feelings for me?" I ask, not wanting to eat my pizza until this conversation is over.

"I lost hope of a future for us."

My heart breaks, and I understand now why she's been so standoffish to me. "Let me prove you wrong."

"You're asking me to jump into the deep end not knowing if I can swim."

"I'm asking you to jump into the deep end and trust me to catch you, not let you drown again."

I could promise to never hurt her again. I don't know what the future holds, but if she gives me another chance, her heart will stay in one piece this time.

She looks at me, lifting her pizza to her mouth. "Friends. We can start as friends."

"I'll take it."

GILLIAN

After two grueling days of taking the bar exam, I had to work the rest of the week, but now it's finally time to enjoy myself. And as luck would have it, tonight is the annual Noughton family Fourth of July pig roast.

"I'm not sure about this." I give myself one last look in my full-length mirror. "It's a little revealing."

"Which is the point." Laurel comes up behind me, looking at me through the mirror.

I'm in a short white dress with a jean jacket and cowgirl boots. "I feel like I'm seventeen again."

"You look gorgeous. Ben is going to be following you around all night." She walks over and grabs her purse.

"Do I want that?"

"I don't know. Maybe I could answer if you'd tell me what's going on with you two."

Our conversation at By the Slice was productive, but Ben made his intentions clear. He wants to start something between us, and I'm not sure what his endgame is. That's Ben, though. The driven part of him sees what he wants and goes after it. He'd never have made it as far as he did if he took no for an answer. He likes the chase, always has. But what happens when he catches me? What happens if that analyst job comes through?

"I agreed to be friends." I didn't want to talk with her about it before since my entire focus had to be on the bar exam, but now that that's past, Ben is at the forefront of my mind.

Laurel blows out a breath, clearly not believing that we can be friends. I'm not sure that I can just be Ben's friend either.

"What am I going to do? We have to work together for the fundraiser, and he confessed that he wants more. A big part of me wanted to saunter around the table and plop myself in his lap."

"But?"

"I don't know..."

"You don't want to be heartbroken again."

I shrug. "Well, sure, who does? But I'm not sure that's it. Nothing can hurt like it did when I was seventeen. I'm tougher now, you know? I can survive on my own. But I don't want to look like some desperate woman or have people say what a fool I am to go back to him."

We plop down on the bed. "Are you telling me you're not pursuing this thing with Ben because you're scared of what other people will say?"

I nod. I've realized that's definitely part of it.

"Gill, that's not like you. Who cares what anyone thinks?"

"It's not just me, though. It's Clayton too, and when I talked to him about the Ben thing, I saw the pain on his face. I have to consider how this will affect him."

She nods a few times. "Clayton will be out of the house in four years. You and Ben have both grown up. And I know he's the love of your life. Don't try to pretend he isn't." She knocks me with her shoulder.

"I've dated people."

She guffaws. "I think you purposely pick people you don't like to go out on dates with."

She has a point. Rarely have I seen someone for more than two dates. I compare every one of them to Ben.

"Let's just go to the party. Stop thinking with your head and start thinking with your heart. Stop getting hung up on the future and just be here now," Laurel says.

"Hate to break it to you, but that whole 'don't think of the future' thing ends when you have a kid. Because every decision I make affects him."

We sit quietly on the bed, and I feel as lost as she looks about this decision. Do I want Ben? Of course I do. I tried the anger route, and that got me nowhere. I tried the "stay away from me, you hurt me too badly" route, and that got me to a pizza place, agreeing to be friends.

"Okay, I'm going to ask you some questions. Don't think, just answer." Laurel faces me on the bed, one leg bent up to rest on the mattress.

"Why?"

"Just do it. Ready?"

I roll my eyes. "Fine."

"You're at the Noughton family Fourth of July pig roast. You see Ben dancing with a gorgeous blonde. What do you do?"

"Ask to cut in."

She laughs but sobers quickly. "You see Ben touch the small of her back to lead her to get a drink."

"Go get a drink too."

"You see Ben go off toward the old barn with her."

I frown. "Fine, point made."

"No, I want to hear what you'd do." Laurel motions with her hand to keep going.

"I'd grab a shovel and hit her over the head with it, then use it to bury her."

"Man... okay. I didn't think we were going to murder the poor woman, but those answers show you where your heart lies."

"No, it's just jealousy. Jealousy isn't rational."

Now Laurel rolls her eyes. "Okay, ready for another round?"

"Laurel..."

"Ben asks you to dance."

"I dance."

"He puts his hand on the small of your back."

"I purposely slow down to feel more of his body against mine."

"He takes you by the hand and leads you to the old barn..."

"I ride him like a cowboy."

She grins. "Atta girl."

I don't mention that our spot isn't the old barn, it's by the river that empties into the lake in the middle of the Noughton property. A spot I hope was never built on as the younger generation has built their houses. I haven't been that far into the property since Ben and I broke up.

"I think you have your answer." She pats my leg. "Now let's go, we're going to be late."

"There's no specific time we need to be there."

"You have to beat the imaginary blonde." She laughs and walks out of my bedroom.

TWENTY MINUTES LATER, LAUREL PARKS HER BABY blue truck with The Sugar Cottage logo on the side of the long country road, along with the rest of Willowbrook's residents.

I pull down my dress. "It's so short."

"Ben will love it," she singsongs.

"Nothing like flashing the entire town."

"Hush. You're beautiful."

We round the back of the Noughton family home, where the festival is held. People say hello to us, and we wave, moving through the adult crowd since most of the kids and teens arrive early and leave early. Clayton came by earlier with Drew and a couple of friends, but he left to go back to Drew's. I feel bad for Betsy because it seems like that's the hang-out house lately.

"Gillian!" Lottie raises her hand, standing off to the side with Sadie Wilkens, Jude's best friend.

"Hey." Laurel hugs Lottie. "Great party as always."

"Hi, Sadie." I hug her briefly, then Laurel and I switch places.

"I worried you weren't coming," Sadie says. "We saw Clayton earlier, and you weren't here. Thought maybe..." She doesn't have to say it. It's the elephant in the room.

"Clayton is too cool to hang with his mom now, Sadie."

She laughs and drinks beer out of her red Solo cup. "Well, you're plenty cool in this crowd."

As she says that, Jude comes up because he's never far from Sadie. "Need another?"

"What, no hello?" Laurel walks over to Jude for a hug.

Jude hugs her, but not a full hug because that's Jude. He's way less affectionate than Ben is. "Gillian," he says and gives me a one-armed hug.

"Done with party prep and ready to party?" I say, all too familiar with the tasks the Noughton boys and their cousins are mandated to do in order for the entire town to enjoy their Fourth of July party.

"Definitely." He downs his beer.

"Gilly Be!" Emmett lifts me from behind before I'm ready. He circles me around and I cringe at Laurel because I'm sure I must be flashing people.

"There's the lovable Noughton." I pat his arms.

A voice clearing interrupts us, and Emmett lowers me to the ground.

"You sayin' I'm not lovable?" Ben asks.

"Oh, look who's jealous." Emmett punches Ben in the chest, and Ben glares at Emmett. "Whoa, man, it's Gilly Be. Cool it with the whole alpha meathead vibe."

"One day you're going to get your ass kicked, Emmett," Jude chimes in.

"In that case." He opens his arms and approaches Sadie. "Sadieeee." He laughs.

Right before he reaches Sadie, Jude steps in front. "Go find a girl for the night."

Emmett pretends to pout and stands over by Lottie.

"Leave him alone," Lottie says.

Everyone knows Lottie is Emmett's protector. She's held that role since they were toddlers.

"Yeah, he can't remember who he's slept with and who he hasn't," Brooks chimes in.

I didn't even notice Brooks right next to Ben. Maybe because I don't want to turn to face Ben. Feeling his eyes on me is enough. Thank you, Laurel.

"Brooks, don't you have to go issue some bullshit tickets?" Lottie shoots back.

He clicks his tongue and shakes his head. "Always Emmett's little bodyguard."

"She's like a quarter of my size. I can take care of myself." Emmett puffs out his chest.

The three of them continue to go at it.

Ben leans down to my ear. "How about we get a drink?"

I have a flashback to my conversation with Laurel in my bedroom. It's the depths of summer, but I still get a rush of shivers throughout my body.

I glance at Laurel since I came with her.

"We've got her. Go." Lottie slides her arm through Laurel's.

"Perfect." Ben places his hand on my back and guides me away from the group. Once we're a distance away, he leans in and says, "If you wore that dress to torture me, it's working."

"I didn't," I lie. I hate lying. I don't want to play games, so I decide to tell the truth. "Laurel picked it out. *She* wanted to torture you."

He chuckles, his hand not leaving my back, and just as I told Laurel, I slow my steps to feel the side of his body along mine. He smells so nice. Not a heavy scented cologne, but soap and his natural scent. The scent I would love to make into a candle one day.

"Remind me to thank her."

There's a makeshift bar with two kegs on either side and two bartenders behind the bar, a stocked table behind them to make drinks.

"Did your dad tell you why they started doing the bar?" I ask.

"Oh, yeah, Jude said Dad insisted on it a couple of years ago because of the high school kids' drinking getting out of hand. Remember how we used to steal beers from the coolers?"

"I do. They caught on, I guess." I chuckle. "I'll just have a beer," I tell the bartender.

"Make it two." Ben digs into his pocket and puts a twenty into the tip jar.

Once we have our beers, Ben leads me away from everyone.

"Shouldn't we go back to our friends?" I ask.

"I thought I was your friend?" He flashes me a smile.

"You are, but..." His flirty personality is shining through, and I'm going to have a hard time not being affected. "Okay, *friend*, what do you want to talk about?"

"Well, *friend*. It's been a long time. I want to hear about what you've been up to."

I pretend to think, staring at the sky and tapping my finger to my lips. "Let's see, I had a baby who is now fifteen. I graduated college to be a court stenographer. I've done that job since then. Eventually decided I wanted to go to law school, which took forever, what with the baby I mentioned. And this week, I took the bar exam."

"You did? I'm so proud of you, Gill."

My stomach swoops at him shortening my name, something he used to always do. He leans in to hug me, and I shamelessly suck in a big breath to catalog his scent.

"These are things friends should tell friends," he says when he pulls away.

"Why?"

"Because a friend would buy you a cake and take you out to celebrate."

"My other friend is a baker, so she'll handle the cake once I get my results."

"And when is that?"

"Six to seven weeks."

He pulls his phone from his back pocket, and his thumbs hammer away on the screen.

"It's rude to text other friends when you're with another friend," I say, wondering who the hell is more important right now.

He peeks up, that smirk in place. "This friend is putting the date in his calendar, so he makes sure not to forget to ask friend about the results. Then this friend can plan a celebration for the friend because they're certain the friend is going to pass."

"Unlike Alondra." I roll my eyes and sip my beer.

"I have a confession." He pockets his phone and rests his elbows on a high-rise table attached to a barrel.

My eyes narrow. "Do I want to know?"

"A friend may have bribed Tori to nominate you to run the football fundraiser." He clenches his teeth.

I should be annoyed, but I'm anything but. I try to remember Laurel's words about how I should stop thinking of the future and worry about the here and now. And here, right now, Ben is in front of me, all smiles and hotness.

"What did said friend promise Tori?" I play along.

"Reserved seats at every Wildcats football game." Seats that we usually auction off for money to the boosters. How he'll swindle this, I'm not sure, but knowing Ben, he'll figure something out.

"I see. And why did the friend do that?"

"Because the friend wanted to be close to you."

I giggle like the old Gillian, and it feels really good. "You're trouble." I sip my beer.

"Your favorite kind of trouble."

God, isn't that the truth.

Chapter Fifteen

BEN

The Noughton pig roast is in full swing now. All the families have left to bathe and put their kids to bed. On the temporary dance floor in the middle of the party, my dad is two-stepping with a redhead, and the older generation sits in chairs along the perimeter. I forgot how peaceful it is here, even in the middle of a party.

"So, friend, tell me about your time away. What's it like being a pro football player?" Gillian draws my attention back to her.

She's blessed me by staying at a table with just me and not seeking out Laurel or any of her other friends.

I was busy bringing a keg to the bar when Gillian walked in. I just about dropped dead when I saw her. The short white dress shows off her tanned legs, which I really want wrapped around me. I'm trying to keep my eyes on hers, but they keep drifting down her body, especially where the dress dips right between her tits.

"It's okay." I twirl my Solo cup, my eyes on the dance floor.

Jude pulls a reluctant Sadie onto the wooden floor, and

they get in sync with my dad and the redhead. I'm not sure about those two. They've been friends all these years, but everyone suspects they're more. How could Jude not have crossed that line by now? Jude isn't nice to anyone but her.

"I can handle it, you know," Gillian says.

I straighten but don't look at her. It's hard for me to tell her all that I experienced when I left her behind.

"Come on, Noughton, your dream came true." She puts her hand on my forearm. "Tell me about it. How excited were you when you got drafted?"

I can't hide my smile. It was one of the best things to ever happen to me. "Pretty great."

"I saw the pictures. Your smile." She doesn't elaborate.

"I think my dad was more excited than me." As much shit as my dad gives me, I never would've made it if not for him pushing me and telling me I was made for greatness. But with his praise came a lot of guilt.

"He brags about you all the time."

My eyes search out Jude. He's smiling with Sadie as she laughs at something he said. When you grow up in a ranching family, it's kind of expected that you'll work the ranch when you get older. My dad took it over from his dad, who took it over from my great-grandfather. I never would've been able to do what I did without Jude and Emmett.

"Sometimes I think it's not real."

"I bet you had to sacrifice a lot," she says.

I turn to Gillian, but she's watching the people circle the dance floor.

"Yeah, I did," I whisper, not thinking about all the parties here that I missed or my time spent in a gym or at training. I sacrificed a future with Gillian, and standing next to her right now, as great as playing pro was, it's hard not to regret that decision.

She must feel my eyes on her because she turns and smiles,

clueless about the real meaning of my words. We're definitely not at a place to discuss that.

"How did you like San Francisco?"

I'm not sure how much she's traveled since I've been gone, but my guess is that a court stenographer doesn't get paid a lot. And she was raising a kid by herself, plus her siblings, so likely not much.

"It took a lot of getting used to. Clemson wasn't a huge city in itself, and even that took getting used to for me. So when I got to San Francisco, I felt pretty lost." I remember the emotions that mixed inside of me that first year. "As a rookie, I was so paranoid about my performance. I didn't want to get cut. And when I sat on the bench for almost the entire first year, it pulled out all these doubts about how I wasn't good enough."

"Then you got your shot."

I blow out a breath, hating that she knows way more about my life than I do hers. But she only knows what everyone else does—what's out there for public consumption. "I did. It was a rough start. I was pretty lonely before I found teammates who turned into friends. I'll always thank Xavier Greene for making me go out with him that first time."

If I had come back here before going to San Francisco, scooped her and Clayton up, and taken them with me, would things have been different? She was my biggest cheerleader, always believing in me.

"But then you soared."

I nod a couple times. "Yeah, and I got a little cocky. A stage I'm not proud of." I'm not going to get into how the fame went to my head. "I needed my dad to bring me down a few pegs. Which he did when he made a surprise visit after the news spread about my partying."

"Good ol' Bruce always guides his boys down the right path."

"That's the truth. I think he gave me a little slack, but I was probably close to losing it all."

"I read the rumors that you weren't playing well, but I never know if I can believe them or not."

"You were checking up on me?"

She sips her drink. "I would tell myself not to do it, but late at night on my phone, I'd just type your name."

"I'm sorry."

"You don't have to apologize for living your life."

I put my hand on the small of her back and step into her, wanting to make sure it's a moment between us when I confess. "You're wrong, Gillian. Because if I was in your position and had to see a picture of you with another man's hands on you, I'm not sure how I would react. I'd probably trash my place or strangle him. It's a toss-up."

She gives me a sad sort of smile. "I never said it was easy. I said you don't have to apologize."

"But I want to. I wish I could say more than just I'm sorry."

She bites the inside of her lip and diverts her eyes from me.

I place my finger under her chin and bring her gaze back to me. "What is it?"

"Had I not felt so lonely and slept with another man, I wouldn't have Clayton. I can't imagine not having him in my life, so I don't regret that it happened, but the truth is that I never should've done it. When we broke up, I felt as lost as you, but I was stuck here with all our memories and people giving me those pitying looks."

I swallow hard, unsure if it's the right thing to do or not but wanting it all out there. "I came back, you know. To try to make it right."

Her head bolts up from staring into her beer. "What?"

"When I first got to Clemson, the distance was harder than I thought it would be. I was far away from home and everything I knew. Every time we talked, it only made me miss you and Willowbrook more. The pressure to not fuck it up because my family had sacrificed so much for me to live out my dream was immense. I would lie awake at night, thinking about coming back to Willowbrook after I made it pro and how we'd move to whatever city drafted me. But I wasn't playing as well as I wanted. The stress consumed me. That night we broke up, I regretted it the minute we hung up. But I didn't think I was going to make it, and every time we talked, my head would get more fucked up because I missed home. I felt like you deserved more than a boyfriend who called you late at night to argue with you and who you never saw. I was holding you back."

I sip my beer, and she places her hand around my waist. "I felt like I was the one holding you back. When did you come home?"

"I came home at Christmas, ready to tell you how sorry I was and that I wanted to make it work. That it was only four years, and yeah, it was going to be hard, but we could figure it out. We just had to have faith in each other and our relationship. That I had finally settled in at Clemson and gotten my head on straight. But when Jude picked me up from the airport, he broke the news about you being pregnant. So I hid out on the ranch until it was time for my flight home and made my family promise not to tell anyone I was there. I pushed you into another man's arms."

A tear slips down her cheek. Every time she cries, the knife in my heart inches deeper.

I wipe it away. "This has all gotten way too serious for a party."

She laughs, not pulling away from me.

I glance at the dance floor, thankful people are giving us privacy. "How about we dance?"

She bites her lip. "If we dance, people will speculate."

"So what?"

"You're right. We're just two friends dancing, right?" Her smile suggests maybe we're stepping out of the friend zone, but I try not to get too excited in case I'm wrong.

"Jude and Sadie are dancing." I take her hand.

She laughs. "I'm not sure about their friend status."

"No one is." I shake my head because my older brother isn't fooling anyone.

I tug on Gillian's hand, and she comes willingly, leaving our beers at the table. My dad side-eyes us, and Sadie smiles as if Jude just proposed while we fall in line with them as they two-step.

"I'm rusty," I admit.

"Then I'll lead you."

My fingers graze her back. Although I love having her this close, I'd love a slow dance so her body could be pressed against mine.

After we've made a couple of circles, we get into the groove. The scene is romantic, with the string lights illuminating the floor and the dark star-filled sky above us. Gillian's beauty still holds me captive, but she's no longer that innocent girl I fell head over heels for. Life has matured her, and I missed it all.

"I'm sorry, Gillian."

She shakes her head. "No more sorrys."

"But—"

"I'm done with us regretting things and feeling bad for what we did to one another when we were young. You're here now. I'm here now. And I know we don't know what the future holds and it's scary, but it has always been you for me. I'm sure people think I'm stupid, but I'm exhausted from fighting my feelings for you."

God damn. Is this it? Is this the moment she gives me an

in? I try to downplay my enthusiasm so I don't scare her off. "You've always been the mature one out of the two of us."

She tips her head toward me. "So no more sorrys, okay?"

"What are you saying, Gillian?"

She remains quiet for another circle around the dance floor, and I think maybe she's not going to answer.

"I'm saying..." She looks around, but no one can overhear us with the music. "Let's see where this goes."

"As far as?"

"Do I really have to spell it out, Noughton?"

"Really?" Hope stirs inside me.

"But." Her eyes scan the area again. "I'm not ready for it to be public. We need to take it slow."

That I can handle. I'll take her any way she'll let me. I stop us from dancing, grab her hand, and drag her off the dance floor.

"Where are we going?"

I take her back to the table. "Pick up your beer and pretend we're taking a break."

Once all eyes have left us, I take her hand again and step back, leading her into the darkness. I stop when we reach the far side of the barn, where a small light shines down. I put one of my hands on the wooden barn above her head and my other one on her waist, peering down at her.

She lifts her head to stare into my eyes. "What are you doing?"

"I'm going to kiss you." I don't want to push her too fast, but after that conversation, I'm starved to feel her lips against mine.

"Friends don't kiss."

"Friends shouldn't wear dresses like this if they don't want to be kissed."

She opens her mouth and shuts it.

"Besides, we just agreed that we're now more than friends.

I think we can strip the word friends from our vocabulary, no?"

"You're talking too much." She grips my shirt with her hands and tugs me down.

I hold her waist, tugging her against me as my lips meet hers. Just like everything when it comes to Gillian, I lose myself.

Chapter Sixteen

GILLIAN

B en grabs my waist, pulling me toward him. I fist his T-shirt and tug him closer. His eyes search mine as everything else blurs around us. I'm desperate to feel the softness of his lips. Our lips collide, and Ben takes control, slowing our pace. He glides his tongue along the seam of my mouth, seeking permission. I open, and we both groan when our tongues tangle.

Time might have stretched between us all these years apart, but I feel as if I'm seventeen again, lying on a blanket by the creek with Ben on top of me. This time, there's no fear for our future. The worst has already happened.

He strips his lips off mine, and I moan from the loss. "Fuck, Gill, I want you so bad."

He places his hands on my cheeks and takes my lips again, our kiss growing hungrier. I release his shirt and run my hands up his expansive chest, around his neck, and through his soft brown hair. I become lost in him as I always did. He pushes me back against the side of the barn, caging me in and pressing himself against me. The hardness through his jeans hits me in the stomach, and my thighs clench together, eager to feel his length grinding between my thighs.

As if he can read my mind, his hands move down my body and around to my ass, grabbing it and pulling up. I go willingly, wrapping my legs around his waist. Too many clothes separate us, but the roughness of his bulging jeans pressed against me with only the barrier of my silk underwear stirs a frenzy inside me.

The tension turns palpable, our hands searching, our tongues warring, our sounds increasing.

"Ben," I sigh, unable to handle much more without having him completely.

"Say it again." His lips trail a path of kisses down my neck. "Say my name again."

"Ben."

"No more Noughton." He doesn't look at me, and my eyes shut.

All the dreams of having him like this again are finally realized, and it's better than I remember. His calloused palms run over my bare skin, and his tongue drags along my flesh. It feels surreal to have him here. He's different but the same.

"No more Noughton," I repeat. I was only doing that to punish him, and we've clearly moved beyond that.

"You have no idea how hard this is for me." His lips continue along my skin, and he props me up higher. His strength only makes me imagine other positions he can get me into.

He kisses his way between my breasts, and I want him to tear this dress off so I can feel his lips on every inch of my skin.

A whistle pulls me out of our bubble.

Ben lowers me and steps back, both of us wiping our mouths.

"Time's up, you little monkeys." It's Brooks, but he hasn't come around the barn.

"Give me a minute," Ben tells him and pushes his body against mine, one arm up on the barn, his body towering over me. I forgot how safe Ben makes me feel.

"You have about two minutes because Bruce is on his way down here with the redhead."

"I guess we shouldn't have picked the make-out area," I say, my fingers running down his broad chest.

"Can we pretend it isn't my dad coming to do what we just did?"

I chuckle and don't mention that Bruce Noughton will probably get further than his son did tonight. "You'll be seeing her tomorrow morning."

He shakes his head and places his finger under my chin, urging me to look at him. "When can I see you alone?"

"Are you asking when you can kiss me again?"

"I'm asking when I can spend time with you. Kissing is a bonus." I smirk, and he chuckles. He lowers his mouth to mine and gives me a sweet kiss. "Come on."

"Bruce!" Brooks says, and our bubble bursts. "Whatcha up to?"

"Brooks. What the hell are you doing alone out here?" Bruce asks.

"I was just staring up at the stars."

"You're never gonna find a woman if your hand is in your own damn pants all the time."

"What?" Brooks screeches. "I wasn't... I mean... damn it."

I cover my mouth to stop my giggle, and Ben leads me by the hand to the other side of the barn.

Lottie and Romy are standing with Laurel by the bar. Laurel's giving me the eye, but I keep my face passive. I'll tell her later what happened tonight with Ben.

We're not out in the open for long before Brooks comes up to us and pushes Ben by the shoulder. "Asshole. Your dad thinks I'm some perv who can't control his hormones for the length of a party."

Ben laughs and steps back. "You took one for the team."

I step forward. "Thank you, Brooks." I go to hug him but step back. "Maybe after you wash your hands."

"Assholes," he mutters and walks away.

"Ah, Brooks, we're joking," Ben calls.

Brooks puts up his hand and heads to the bar since he's like a magnet to Lottie nowadays, or maybe it's been for forever. It's hard to remember.

"Where's Clayton tonight?" Ben asks.

I pull out my phone, feeling like a neglectful parent. There's a text asking if he can spend the night at Drew's. But I'm not ready to sleep with Ben yet. "He's at Drew's, but..."

Ben shakes his head. "No, I didn't think... although when you're ready, you just have to tell me, or put your hand on my dick, or get naked. I'll take any of those options."

I giggle and step toward him before realizing I can't. There are a lot of people here.

"Let's go have some fun with our friends since you have the night free." He puts out his arm for me to head toward the bar.

"That I can do."

We walk over to the large group of people from our generation: Ben's two sets of cousins from his dad's sisters who have all built businesses on the ranch, along with Brooks and Laurel, Jude, and of course Sadie. Emmett is surely out in the field with some girl.

Ben gets me a new beer and raises his cup. "To being home."

Everyone clinks their Solo cups and takes a sip.

ALL THE TABLES AROUND THE DANCE FLOOR ARE separated by generations. Ben's dad, aunts, uncles, and their friends are spread along two tables. Our age group is at one, while another table is filled with the elderly people from town. Our table is filled with red Solo cups. It feels as though I'm a part of a family again. Just that quick.

"So, you're going to be the high school football coach?" Romy asks.

"It appears that way." Ben sips his drink, looking uncomfortable with the discussion.

"I'd assist, but I'm way too busy at the station." Brooks smacks Ben on the back. He somehow swindled the spot next to Lottie.

"Busy getting coffee." Lottie never denies an opportunity to give Brooks shit.

"I have to stay awake."

"Because your job is so strenuous? You need caffeine to keep you up because it's boring. I'm pretty sure the NYPD don't need coffee to 'stay awake.'" She puts stay awake in air quotes.

"Can we please discuss the softball team this year?" Jude interrupts because those two will go on forever.

"I heard Walker Matthews just hired some guy that was all-state in baseball." Romy sips her drink as though she shouldn't have shared, but it's too juicy not to.

"I heard." Jude shakes his head. "I swear Wild Bull Ranch only hires someone if they can play on their team."

"But we have Benny now!" Brooks smacks Ben on the back. "I'm sure with all that muscle you have, you'll be hitting homers."

Ben chokes on his beer, coughing for a moment. "I didn't say I was playing."

Jude stares across the table. "You are."

"I have a lot on my plate."

Ben has a point, but still, why would he not play on the Plain Daisy Ranch softball team? Every year, all the ranches play against one another, and although you don't win anything tangible, it's holding the title that matters.

"You're fucking kidding me, right?" Jude is visibly upset, sitting up straighter, eyes locked on Ben.

So much between them needs to be aired out, but they're both too proud to do it.

Sadie puts her hand on Jude's forearm.

"Fine. I'll do it." Ben shrugs.

"You were joking, right?" Brooks leans in and asks, because it would've been a dick move if Ben didn't join the team.

"I didn't know if you had room for me," Ben says, and I take note to ask him about that later.

"There's always room, especially for someone who's going to get us the win," Brooks says.

Jude stands so abruptly his chair falls behind him onto the ground. He storms off. Sadie gives us all a wan smile, following him.

"Let's do shots." Brooks stands and heads to the bar.

"We're old, we don't do shots," Lottie hollers after him, but we all know she'll do the shot.

Other conversations pick up around us, and I lean into Ben. "Why would you not want to play on the team?" I whisper.

His hand slides under the table, landing on my knee. When he runs his hand up and down my leg, he ignites the flame inside me that had died to burning embers after our make-out session.

He looks at the empty spot Jude left. "I don't want to step on anyone's toes, and I don't want the expectations Brooks just put on me."

I can see that. Jude started the softball league after he graduated high school, so it's always been his thing. And everyone thinks Ben will go out there and dominate just because he was a professional athlete.

Brooks brings the shots over and passes them out. "To beating Walker Matthews and Wild Bull Ranch this year."

Everyone cheers and downs the shot.

I cough because I haven't had straight alcohol in years.

"That means you need another, Gillian." Brooks leaves to go back to the bar again.

"I do not. I have a son to get home to."

Ben gives me side-eye since he knows Clayton is staying at Drew's.

Someone brings up high school, and memories flow out of everyone. Each of us has our fair share. The drinks flow, and Brooks keeps bringing shots.

I start to feel buzzed and stop pushing Ben's hand off my leg. I uncross my legs, and his fingers slide down to the inside of my thigh. Everyone is too busy and too drunk to notice what's happening.

Lottie and Brooks continue their banter. Laurel and Romy talk about some Bridezilla and her cake demands for an upcoming wedding at The Knotted Barn. And I'm lost, my head growing fuzzier from alcohol and lust.

I don't want this moment to end. I want to stay here forever. Us with our friends from high school, as if the fourteen-year gap never happened. If Ben had stayed or I had gone to meet him, would we still be here? I can't confidently answer that question.

I look at Ben when Brooks tells everyone about how Ben and I would swim to the other side of the quarry around a rock outcropping and how we weren't fooling anyone. Ben smiles at me, and his hand slides a little farther up my leg, dangerously close to the barrier of my underwear.

Drinking was not a good idea. I'm losing my inhibitions, and there are a lot of witnesses, but I find I don't care.

There's another round of shots—this time from Lottie, because once she gets going, she turns into the ringleader. She and Brooks are so similar, and they don't even realize it.

Pretty soon, the lights above me blur, and my head spins.

"Um..." I mumble and stand. "I need water."

"Whoa. I'll get it." Ben's hands land on me, and I fall into them and laugh.

Then everything goes black.

Chapter Seventeen

BEN

"Oh shit, she's drunk," Laurel says.

I saw it coming, with Gillian's eyes turning glassy and her letting me touch her under the table. Everyone knew where my hand was, I'm sure. But I didn't imagine she was this drunk.

"I don't feel good," Gillian slurs, her hand over her stomach.

"Thanks, Brooks." I scowl at him.

Laurel stands, and I already know she's about to take Gillian from me. I put up my hand. "I've got her."

"No really. I drove her here," Laurel says.

"And I'll get her home and take care of her."

Laurel hems and haws and looks at Romy as if she needs her permission.

"Laurel, I threw the shots over my shoulder and had a total of one beer hours ago."

"What a waste of alcohol." Brooks shakes his head at me.

"Someone, put him in my bed tonight?" I ask, nodding at my friend.

Jude finally showed back up after his fit. I'd never confess to him that I don't want to barge in on his thing, that maybe he prefers something without me being involved. Ever since I left town, I've felt his resentment like oil coating my skin whenever we're around each other.

"We'll take care of him. You take care of her." Sadie nods toward Gillian, who is using me like a support beam.

I pick Gillian up over my shoulder.

"Ben!" Laurel shouts and rushes over. She looks at the group, which has already gone back to talking and laughing with each other. "You guys... I mean, I'd be a shit friend if I didn't ask... I know you two disappeared for a while."

I understand Laurel's point, and I'm thankful that Gillian has Laurel to look out for her. Especially since I've been away. But I'm back now. "We're going to give it a go and see what happens."

A smile forms on her lips but dies quickly. She points at me and narrows her eyes. It's almost comical coming from Laurel. What is she going to do—buttercream me to death?

"Okay, Ben, but I swear if anything happens to her, I can kill you, cut you into small pieces, and bake you into a cake."

I raise my eyebrows, and she laughs.

"You know I'd never do anything to..."

Her eyebrows raise, and I nod.

"At least take my car. She's not going to want your truck parked outside her house." She rushes back to the table and digs into her purse, then shoves her keys in my hand.

"You have nothing to worry about."

Her shoulders relax, and she walks around to my back. "Gillian, Ben's going to take you home. Are you okay with that?"

"Why are you asking her permission? She's drunk."

"Of course," Gillian says. "We're probably going to have sex, but don't tell anyone," she whispers.

I try not to laugh, but I fail miserably.

"You're not going to have sex." Laurel's voice is stern.

"Why not?" Gillian sounds upset, so I swing around.

"We're leaving. Jude? Sadie?" They look up, and I point at Laurel to make sure they take care of her too.

Although they're only a year older than the rest of us, we all treat Jude and Sadie like the older, wiser ones who have their shit together. Sadie nods. Thankfully, she's a nurturer.

I walk around the house and out to the road, then press the key fob to Laurel's truck. She's got to be kidding me. I thought she had another vehicle and just made deliveries in this one. It's a powder blue truck with a pink and white logo on the side.

Gillian's head lands on the headrest, and she circles it to look at me while I put her seat belt on. "Why did Laurel say that? That was mean."

"Laurel meant because you're drunk. She doesn't want me to take advantage of you."

She wraps her arms around my neck, pulling me toward her. "I'm not that drunk. Take advantage of me."

I'd like to record her so she can hear the slur in her words in the morning.

"Let's get you home." I kiss her forehead and unwind her arms from around my neck.

On the ride home, Gillian goes from having her eyes shut to sleeping. This is a first. I've never seen her this drunk, but she deserved to blow off steam after the bar exam.

I pull into her driveway and park the truck next to her car in front of her two car garage, then I get out and walk around to her side.

"Gill?" I nudge her awake and undo her seat belt. "I need the keys."

Her eyes spring open, and she stares at me for a minute. "Ben?" She touches her lips. "Was it a dream?" Both hands touch my face, patting it all over. "You feel real."

"Yeah, I'm real."

"Okay." She tries to climb out of the truck, and I grab her waist. She falls into my body. "You're so cute." Her hands slide down my chest and rest on my belt, her fingers dipping under.

"We gotta get you inside. I need your house keys."

She looks around. "I have a keypad."

Great. I hope she remembers the code.

We walk up to her front door, though by walk, I mean Gillian weaves. She trips up her porch step, and I yank her back into me before she face-plants.

She stares at the keypad for a second, then at me, giggling. "I don't remember it." She covers her mouth, and her fingers go to the keypad and back to her mouth. "Huh."

"Do you have any other way to get in?"

She looks around.

"A key under the mat? One of those hidden rock things?"

She shakes her head. "It'll come to me." Her head rocks back, and a gurgling sound escapes her throat.

"I tell you what." I turn her body around and lower her to the step. "You sit here. I'm going to figure this out."

"My hero." She laughs and slumps over so she's resting on the porch post.

I walk around the property, trying every window of the ranch house. Nothing is unlocked—which I'm happy about, but still. The patio door is locked tight with a bar across the side. When I get back, she's asleep, a light snore echoing through the darkness.

I go to the keypad, determined to figure this out.

I try her birthday but get a red light. I'm wondering how many chances I get before it locks me out. I have no idea what Clayton's birthday is, so that's not an option. There's no chance, but I type in my birthday anyway, not surprised when it turns red.

"Fuck," I say, loudly enough that she startles awake.

"Whatcha doing?" she asks.

"Trying to get into your house." I bend down to her level, moving my hand to tuck a strand of hair behind her ear. When I do, she flinches and draws back. That's the second time she's done that, and I do not like where my mind goes as to why she might react that way. "Gillian, do you remember your code to get in your house?"

"070509."

"Really?" I ask, not sure if I can believe her, but I enter it anyway.

The light turns green. I rack my mind for the meaning of the numbers. It can't be Clayton's birthday because he was born in 2010, if my math is correct. Maybe they're just random.

I lift Gillian and carry her in fireman style since she's passed out again.

Her house is neatly decorated with minimal clutter. The pictures adorning the walls are of Clayton, or her and Clayton. Two with her younger half-siblings, Briar and Koa. Her couch looks comfy, with a television on the opposite wall. The space speaks Gillian.

I take her into the master bedroom, strip off her jean jacket and her boots, then open the covers and slide her under them before turning her on the side and tucking her back in.

Not wanting to lie on the bed, I strip down to my boxer briefs, grab the blanket from the end of her bed, and sit on the small chair in the corner of the room that barely fits me so I can watch her sleep.

Eventually, my eyes betray me, the day of completing my dad's long chore list for the party getting the better of me. It's when I'm dozing off that my memory triggers. 070509. Her key code is the day I left Willowbrook.

❧

I AWAKEN TO THE AUTOMATIC LOCK OF THE FRONT door sliding open. Gillian is still in bed, the blankets flung off, and her legs spread open. The dress rose through the night, offering me a glimpse of her white silk underwear. Fucking hell.

"Mom!" Clayton calls. "Laurel!"

Shit. I grab the blanket and cover Gillian, so she doesn't have to be embarrassed.

"Gill." I nudge her.

She mumbles something and rolls over.

I grab my pants, putting one leg in while whispering her name over and over. I'm trying to get dressed so fast, I lose my footing and land with a loud thud on the bedroom floor.

"Mom?" Clayton stands in the doorframe, staring at me. He's definitely not pleased.

"Hey, Clayton," I say from the floor with one leg in my pants and the other one out.

"What are you doing here?" He scans me, probably to make sure his eyes aren't deceiving him. "Mom!"

Gillian jolts awake, looks at him, and bolts up in the bed. "Clay!" She lifts the blankets to cover herself, then peeks down to see how she's dressed. There's a look of relief on her face.

"What's this?" Clayton asks, motioning to me.

Gillian looks at me, her forehead scrunching. I slide my leg into my jeans and stand. Gillian's eyebrows rise as if she's reminding me I'm still shirtless. I grab my shirt off the floor and toss it over my head.

"Um..." Her cheeks are so red, you'd think she just ran through the desert.

"I gave your mom a ride last night."

Clayton's expression transforms from anger to disgust. "Gross."

"I meant a ride home. I gave her a ride home."

Gillian bites her lip.

"Where's Laurel? Her truck is outside," Clayton says.

Gillian's gaze shoots to me. She must not remember. Not that I thought she would.

"She lent me her truck to drive your mom home," I say.

He turns his attention to his mom, then scoffs, storming off. What I assume is his bedroom door slams seconds later.

"I cannot believe this. How sloppy I was." Gillian has her head in her hands.

"You didn't throw up," I say to try to make her feel better.

She stands from the bed and shuts the door quietly. "No. Sloppy as far as being a mom and letting my son see you in boxer briefs and me hungover in my bed with the clear presumption that we slept together."

"We didn't."

She points at the door. "He doesn't know that."

"Want me to tell him?"

"No. The damage is done, and you need to leave while I talk to him." She opens the door and grabs a sweatshirt out of a drawer.

When I don't move, she takes hold of my arm and leads me out of the room.

"I'll call you later," she whispers, continuing to walk toward the front door.

"I like your house."

She stops at the door, opening it as if I can't do that myself. "Thanks?"

"I'm sorry. I didn't mean to start something."

Her shoulders relax. "It's my fault. You don't have kids. How would you know?" It's not a knife she's poking me with, but it feels that way.

"I just wanted to be here if you got sick." Guilt curdles my stomach.

"I know. I know. But you have to leave now." She nudges me toward the door.

"Jeez, I feel so used," I joke, hoping it lightens the mood.

She smiles and stands in the house while I'm on the porch. I'm worried this will forever be us—sneaking around, never free to just enjoy each other. "Thank you for taking care of me. Bye, Ben."

She moves to shut the door, but I put my hand on it. "Wait... can I have your number?"

She smiles and shakes her head. "You already have it."

"I do?" After all these years, she's never changed her number? Don't I feel like an asshole for never using it.

"Bye, Ben." She shuts the door in my face.

I stare at the keypad, telling myself I need two questions answered by Gillian, but one is way more important than the other. I want to know who hurt her and where I can find him. Because there's something behind her flinches. I know there is.

Chapter Eighteen

GILLIAN

I throw on my sweatshirt and walk down the hallway. How do I explain this situation to Clayton? He already doesn't like Ben.

I knock on his door. "Clay?"

"Don't worry about it, Mom."

I open the door and peek in. He's sitting in his gaming chair, ready to boot up a game.

"Can you give me a minute?"

"I don't care."

I pick up his clothes that are strewn on the floor and toss them in his laundry bin. Usually I'd be on him to do it, but the mom guilt is extra fierce this morning. "It's not what you think."

He glances over his shoulder, looks me up and down, and turns around. "I'm old enough that you don't have to sugarcoat it. It was pretty obvious what was going on."

"It was the Fourth of July party at the Noughtons'." I stop. Probably should've taken time to figure out my wording.

"I know. I was there before you, remember?"

"Well, at night, a lot of the adults get together. I'm not

proud of it, but I drank too much, and Ben drove me home." I make his bed, tucking the sheets in tight like he likes.

"Why'd he drive you home?"

"I'm not sure. To be honest with you, I don't remember." I cringe. "But I'm sure I probably wanted him to. Ben and I..."

"I know. You told me already how he left you here." The hurt in his tone is something I'm familiar with. It's the same tone when we discuss his father.

"He left to fulfill his dream."

"And in exchange, he left you behind. He could've come back for you."

"Look at me, Clayton," I say, but he doesn't.

He continues to pretend that this is going to be a quick "you're not doing your chores" conversation. But this is so much more.

"Clay."

He spins on his chair to face me. "I'm not sure what you expect me to say. He's going to be the football coach. He's going to be involved in my life for the next four years, if he sticks around."

I don't mention that it depends on whether we do too. Now is not the time to talk about us moving.

"And I already don't like him," Clay adds.

"You don't have to like him, but you should know that I've decided to forgive him."

"You what?" His voice gets louder. "How could you?"

"It's complicated, and I don't expect you to understand. You will when you get older. We were young and—"

"Are you going to date him?"

That's the question. Before the alcohol haze of last night, that searing kiss comes to mind. I'm pretty sure I said we'd try. And although I don't want the town to know and had plans of keeping Clayton out of it for a while, that ship has sailed. I told my son I'd never lie to him, and I meant it. If I lie to him, he'll start lying to me, and that's not the relationship I want with my son.

"I might. But I really don't want anyone else to know."

He shakes his head, resting his forearms on his thighs. "So you'll be his little secret?"

"No. It was by my request. I don't want to be the topic of gossip."

"Or you're afraid that when he leaves, like we all know he will, you'll be embarrassed that you walked right back into his arms."

Damn, that hurt. Maybe this whole being truthful thing is overrated.

"Maybe that is part of it. I'm sure you don't want to hear this, Clayton, but Ben has always held a piece of my heart."

"Excuse me while I throw up."

"That's a warning. You don't have to agree with my decisions, but you *will* respect me."

"Sorry," he mumbles.

I pat the spot next to me on the bed, and with exaggerated movements only a teenager can pull off, he comes over to me. I take his hand. "I know you're worried that he's going to hurt me, and I can't tell you I'm not scared. But one thing I've learned is that not everyone gets a tomorrow. I tried to push him away when he came back, but I don't want to anymore."

"You don't have to—"

"Just listen for a second, okay? Let Mom give you a little advice even though you know everything."

He stops talking, staring down at the floor.

I squeeze his hand that's now bigger than mine. "I'd rather have Ben for however long I have him than pass up this opportunity that might be our last chance."

"And where do I fit?"

My head rocks back. "Look at me."

He peeks up at me through his dark eyelashes.

"You're always number one. No one ever comes before you."

"Not even Ben?"

"Not even Ben," I repeat.

He sits there for a moment, and I prepare myself for a tough question because I know this kid. He doesn't pull any punches.

"Then why do you want to keep it a secret? I mean, you sound like you're fine if he leaves. Why spend the time you have sneaking around?"

I hate it when he's smarter than me. "I don't have an answer for that."

"You mean I stumped you?" He laughs.

I remove my hand from his and put my arm around his shoulders. "I guess you did, but until I'm ready, can we keep this our secret?"

"As long as we can end this conversation."

"Sure."

"And you're not going to make me have dinner with him and stuff, right?"

I huff. "You're an important part of my life, and I'd like you two to get to know one another. But I'll give you time to process first. Does that sound okay?"

He stands and grabs his phone. "Fine. I gotta shower."

I get up off the bed. When did he get so tall? "Hey, I want a hug."

He comes over and hugs me. Nothing's better than when your kid squeezes you tightly. "Jeez, you reek of alcohol."

I swat him as he jumps out of my arms, laughing. "How do you know what alcohol smells like?"

"Gotta go." He rushes out of the room.

"Clayton!"

He shuts his door, and I shake my head. I grab his laundry to start the wash.

As I'm walking by the bathroom door, he opens it a sliver. "No, Mom, I'm not drinking."

"Didn't think you were," I say, walking away. Damn, that picked up my heart rate though.

I'm putting the laundry in the washer when my phone dings. I pull it out of the hoodie pocket and see a number I don't know.

> Lose the number creep.

I laugh to myself and finish starting the laundry.

The phone rings with the same number.

"It's me, Ben," he says before I can say hello.

"I was joking."

He doesn't laugh, and he's quiet for a moment. "I have to clean up after the party today. Will you give me some incentive to get it done early and go out with me tonight?"

I think about Clayton and how I don't ever want him to feel abandoned. And he doesn't want Ben over here just yet. But a big part of me wants to see Ben.

"I'm not sure I can tonight." As I say that, my phone dings with a message. "Hold on."

I bring my phone down and see a text from Clayton asking to go to the movies with friends tonight. I guess that makes my night free, so I text back and tell him he can go.

"Turns out I am available," I tell Ben.

"Great. Do you want to meet somewhere? I know you don't want people knowing about us."

"Um..." I think about what Clayton said, and he's right. If I hide this relationship, what does that say about my faith in Ben? "You can pick me up."

"Are you sure?"

I nod, but he can't see me. I'm still convincing myself. "I'm sure."

"Great. I'll pick you up at six." The excitement in his voice puts flutters in my belly.

"Okay."

Bruce calls Ben in the background as though he's a teenager again. I love Bruce.

"Gotta go, the drill sergeant calls."

"Okay, bye."

"Bye."

I hang up and press the phone to my chest.

"Oh man, are you going to have that look on your face every time you talk to him?" Clayton's wearing only a towel, droplets of water dripping from his hair.

"Where are your clothes?"

"In the hamper." He points to the empty basket on the dryer.

"You have no clean clothes?"

He shrugs. "I wanted to wear my football shirt tonight."

"It's in the washer now. Surely, you have something to put on in the meantime."

He walks toward his bedroom.

"Hey, Clay?"

He turns around.

"Who are you going out with tonight? Drew?"

"And others." He smirks.

I smile at him. "Who?"

"Well, I'm taking your advice. I asked Kait if she wanted to go, and her parents will only let her go in a group, so we're all going."

I smile that he took a chance and it paid off for him. "Well, be careful."

"You too. I heard you making plans. Don't go making me a big brother." His entire body shakes, and he walks out of the laundry room.

I love that kid's resilience.

Chapter Nineteen

BEN

I haven't been this nervous since my first day with the Kingsmen. Walking out to the high school football field with all the boys in their shorts and shirts, sitting down and waiting to hear what I have to say is messing with my nerves. If I'm honest with myself, it's more the fact that Clayton is among the boys.

Gillian told me she told him about us, but she's giving him time to process. I'm not a parent, so I'm happy to support whatever she feels is right for this situation.

Willowbrook High has two teams, which is more than most small towns. Freshmen mostly play junior varsity, and everyone else plays varsity. The only reason is that the freshmen aren't usually big enough to play varsity. Willowbrook would be better off making it all varsity, but I understand the concern. I'll be coaching varsity but filling in for Coach Marks means I oversee the entire program.

Standing in front of the group, I can see the divide. Junior varsity players sit on one side and varsity players on the other. I always hated this mentality when I was a Wildcat.

"First line of business," I say. "Junior varsity stand."

All the junior varsity players stand.

"Varsity stand."

They do the same.

"Shoulder to shoulder, each group line up on either side of the fifty-yard line."

They all do as asked, which doesn't surprise me. Coach Marks runs a tight program. Some of the players I went to college with had to be beaten into shape by the coaches for lack of trying, lack of respect, and just not knowing when to shut their damn mouths.

"I'm going to come down the line. Varsity, you will count one, two as I go down the line. Understood?"

"Yes, Coach," they all say.

I start with the end closest to me and go down the line, separating them into groups of two. They're all clearly confused. This isn't something Coach Marks has ever done, but I'm hoping it will help the overall comradery of the team.

"Okay, each group of two has a junior varsity player in front of them, right?"

"Yes, Coach," they say in unison.

"Step forward, junior varsity members, to be with the twosome in front of you."

Even the assistant coaches look confused, questioning what I'm doing at this point.

"Junior varsity, these are your new football mentors. They've been through the program and know how it works. Varsity players, you will befriend your junior varsity player. You will share your knowledge and help them in any way you can. All varsity players will go to the junior varsity games and support the team, and vice versa. Have I made my expectations clear?"

"Yes, Coach."

"There's no us and them. We're all Wildcats. Understood?"

"Yes, Coach."

"Please don't do something that makes me have to address this again."

"Yes, Coach."

The varsity players eye one another, so I'll definitely have to have my ears open during practices.

"Let's start with running. Get going, and we'll tell you when to stop." I blow my whistle.

There're a lot of grunts, but they get in a line and start running around the field.

Coach Smith comes up to me. He's my offensive line assistant, and, oddly, he coached me. "I'm impressed already."

"Well, I always hated how junior varsity felt like they should kiss the asses of the varsity players. Sure, they deserve their respect, but they'll get that if they actually mentor the JV players."

"Speaking as the junior varsity coach, I love it." Coach Reyes joins our group, setting up the ladder drill for the running backs.

"Let's just hope it works."

I watch the boys, more spaced out now as the faster, better conditioned players move to the front and the slower ones pull up the rear. I've never seen a lineman who can run as fast as the other players.

One kid I don't know is at the very back. He's overweight and struggling with the run. He's a senior, if memory serves, from the roster that Coach Marks shared with me that included everyone's pictures. This right here will show if my words from earlier made any impact. How well can these boys work together?

"I told Harris to condition after last season," Coach Smith says, shaking his head.

"And look who's leading the pack." Coach Reyes nods. "My new wide receiver."

I follow his line of vision to Clayton, who's in the lead. He's about to lap Harris.

"Are you sure he shouldn't be a running back?" I ask.

"The kid's got hands. Why do you think everyone in town thinks he's your kid?"

I whip my head toward Coach Reyes, and Coach Smith makes a sound like he's such an idiot.

"He's good?" I ignore the part about Clayton being mine. It hurts enough that he isn't. I wasn't there for Gillian when she needed me most.

As far as I know, no one knows who Clayton's father is. I've never wanted to ask, and from the rumors in town, it's never been shared. Which means Gillian has kept it to herself all these years. I wonder if Clayton knows who his father is. Was his father ever around? So many questions I need to ask Gillian, but I've been trying to go at it slowly. I know it's a touchy subject for her.

"He could probably be varsity, but we need him on JV," Coach Reyes says.

It's ultimately my decision, but even if Clayton has the hands, his thin frame will be a detriment to him on varsity.

"Give him time to come up. That's the best decision. But make sure he's hitting the weight room. The kid needs some muscle," I say.

The players hit Harris on the ass as they pass, each one razzing him about being slow. That is not the mentality I want for this team. Clayton is about to pass Harris a second time, but he slows to a jog.

He doesn't smack Harris's ass or laugh at Harris. Clayton jogs alongside him, and I can tell from the change in expression on Harris's face that whatever Clayton's saying is encouraging. It reminds me of Gillian.

"What's he like?" I ask the coaches. I catch them eyeing one another.

"From what I hear, he's a good kid. Has a tight-knit group of friends. Respectful to his teachers," Coach Smith says.

"Smart too. Honor roll type," Coach Reyes adds.

I watch Clayton for another second. A feeling of pride washes over me, and I'm unsure why. He's not my son and I didn't raise him, but the woman I love did, and she did an amazing job, which doesn't surprise me in the least.

I tell Clayton and Harris to stop and tell the rest to keep going. I debate calling out Clayton, although he deserves the shout-out for being a team player. I don't want people to think I'm favoring him, but he should be recognized for what he did.

After another lap, I tell them all through my megaphone to stop at the goalpost. Each of them stops, grabbing their waters, and walking around to cool down.

"You're all running for not being team players. You've heard the phrase you're only as strong as your weakest player. Instead of building up someone who is struggling, you chose to make fun of him. This is not acceptable. I'm sure some of you have missed a pass, missed a field goal, or read the play wrong. You already knew what you did wrong, didn't you? How helpful is it if I yell at you for your mistake?"

They all remain silent.

"Would you rather me work with you at the next practice? Talk about what went wrong, give you help on improving that skill?"

No one says anything again, but there are nods.

I love Coach Marks, but he's definitely got an old-school coaching style.

"From this point forward, we boost one another up the way Clayton was doing. If a play doesn't go down like we planned or if the ball slips out of your hands, we pat our teammate on the back and tell them next time. Do I make myself clear?"

"Yes, Coach."

I don't expect anything to change overnight, but hopefully by the end of the season, it will sink in. "Now split up into position drills."

They all jog to their designated spots on the field, and I grab my clipboard to jot down notes on what needs improvement.

"Must be nice that the coach is your mom's boyfriend," one of the players sneers at Clayton.

Maybe I should've listened to my gut and not pointed him out.

Clayton side-eyes me on his way to the area for the wide receivers. I want to see what he has. I pick up a ball from the bag.

"Adams!" I yell and show him the ball.

He nods and jogs, glancing back at me. I throw it, and he catches the ball with ease. His skills are on point with the way he cradles and holds it into his body. I'm sure someone before Coach Marks must have worked with him. Could it have been his dad?

Practice goes well, and I get a good feeling about the team and the players' skills. We have a solid group of boys, but I still need to do some scouting on the other teams to see how we compare. It's been a long time since I've been to a high school football game.

On my way off the field, with my bag swung over my shoulder, I spot Gillian in her car, waiting by the curb. I walk over and tap on the window.

She startles, but the smile I get when she sees that it's me is what dreams are made of. She rolls down her window. "Hey, how was practice?"

I rest my arms on the inside of her car door. "Better now."

"You and your lines." She playfully rolls her eyes.

"Hey, are you available Friday night?"

She nods. "I'm sure I probably am. Clayton always seems to have plans."

The loudness of the boys talking draws my attention to them coming out of the building. "Great. I'll pick you up at six."

"Okay. What should I wear?"

"Nothing."

She laughs. "Well then." Her own eyes stray to the boys.

"I probably shouldn't kiss you."

"Probably not." She slides her tongue across her bottom lip.

"You say no, and then you're going to tempt me?"

She laughs.

The passenger door opens. I was too distracted by her to realize Clayton was already here. A few of the players walk by me, each one glancing in our direction.

"Can we not?" Clayton says. "I already got shit from everyone for getting called out."

Gillian glances at me, then at Clayton. "You're the one who said not to live in secret."

"Jesus, Mom, can we please just go?"

Gillian smiles and puts the car in drive.

"Hey, Clayton, I'm sorry for calling you out, but what you did is the type of mentality I want the team to have. It's an admirable quality, and you should feel good about yourself."

"What did you do?" Gillian asks, looking between us.

"Oh. My. God. Can we go?"

"Owen Harris was struggling with the run, and Clayton jogged alongside him, encouraging him," I say.

"Oh." Gillian puts her hand over her heart. "I'm proud of you, Clay."

"Can I be rewarded by getting out of here?" He slides down in his seat.

"I guess I'd better go." She purses her lips at me and drives off.

I watch their taillights turn out of the school lot. I've never wanted to be in a car so badly in my life.

Chapter Twenty

GILLIAN

On Wednesday night, the first softball game between the ranches is held under the lights at the high school. Of course it's Plain Daisy Ranch against Wild Bull Ranch, the two biggest rivals of all the ranches that play in the league.

My doorbell rings as I'm grabbing my purse. "Clay, I'll be home later," I shout.

He took a shower after practice, so he walks out wearing just his shorts. It's been three days since football camp started, and since the first day, Ben has kept his distance when I'm picking Clayton up from practice. I'm thankful he understands what it's like for Clayton.

"You going on a date with Coach Noughton?"

"Softball game. Want to come? It's a big one."

"A bunch of old guys trying to live out their glory days? No thanks." Clayton grabs a bag of chips and heads down the hall.

"Love you," I yell.

"Love you too. Hope no one breaks a hip." He laughs.

Kids. It's like they don't realize that one day if they're lucky, they'll be older too.

The camera on my doorbell chimes, and when I open the front door, Ben stands there wearing shorts and a blue T-shirt that says Plain Daisy Ranch with a swoosh under it.

"Nice shirt," I say.

"Just got it." He turns around, and I see that the back says Noughton with a number two underneath.

I laugh.

"I think Jude likes being Noughton number one. You ready?" he asks.

"Yep."

"Does Clayton want to come?" he asks.

"We're not there yet." I shut the door behind me, rising on my tiptoes. "But I can kiss you now."

He wraps his arm around my waist, pulling me into him, and our lips meet in a too-short kiss.

"I can see you." Clayton's voice comes out of the camera. "And so can Mrs. Davenport and her corgi."

Ben and I look toward the sidewalk, and sure enough, Mrs. Davenport has a huge smile on her face while her dog squats in my yard, doing his business.

"Thanks, Clay." I put my hand over the camera and kiss Ben quickly again.

"Did you forget there's sound too?" Clay says.

"Bye, Clay." I wave goodbye to him through the camera.

We walk out to the truck, and Ben opens the door for me. I rise on my toes again and kiss him. The smile he shoots back melts my heart. Was I a fool to think we could take this slow?

Once he's in the cab and the key is in the ignition, I take a moment to admire him. "I say we go make out and skip the game."

His eyes roam up and down my body. My cutoff shorts show a lot of leg, and I have a tighter T-shirt that reads Plain Daisy Ranch. I got it from The Harvest Depot years ago.

"Tempting. We can make out after, though. Do you have a curfew?"

I giggle like the girl I feel like when I'm around him. "No curfew."

"Then it's a date."

"We have a date Friday," I say.

He pulls out of the driveway and drives toward the high school. "I'd see you every day of the week if I could."

My stomach flips over with a stir of flutters.

"How is Clayton enjoying practice?" he asks.

"He doesn't say much. Says Coach Reyes likes him."

"He's really talented." Ben glances at me before looking back at the road. "Who did he work with? Seems like he must have been working with someone, unless it's natural talent."

Now my stomach twists. I knew this would come up at some point. "Um..."

"Was it his dad who worked with him?"

I laugh. "No." The idea of that is preposterous.

He parks in the high school lot and cuts the engine. We're a little early, but the Wild Bull Ranch players are already practicing.

"You don't have to tell me. I'm just wondering how much Clayton's dad is in the picture."

I fiddle with my hands in my lap. "He's not."

I knew eventually this topic would surface and I've pondered what to tell him. Clayton doesn't even know who his father is. But Ben does.

"Do you want to know who it is?" I ask. "You must. The entire town has always wondered. Most will always believe he's yours even though I've said he isn't."

Ben puts his hand on my leg and shakes it a little. "Yeah, I want to know, but not if you're not ready to tell me. I'll never push you to tell me anything."

I turn to face him, knowing if we're moving toward a future he has to know. "It's Waylon Knight."

He strips his gaze off me and my heart plummets. Waylon was in Jude's year and was never seen as a great man in Willowbrook. Even in his teens, he was always getting into trouble. After he graduated, he never amounted to anything other than an exceptional bar patron.

"Knight?" he asks with disbelief in his tone. "I didn't think... I mean, I thought he left town after graduation."

"He came back after you went to college. His grandmother passed, and he had to settle her affairs. One night, about a month after we broke up, I went to a bar in Hickory to meet Laurel, but when I got there, she messaged to say she'd gotten hung up at school. He and I met up and swapped 'sorry for me' stories."

"Yeah, I don't want to hear anymore," he says, his voice tight.

I worry that maybe I just ruined his night. He already feels the pressure of playing well tonight. "I didn't mean to upset you."

"You didn't. I'm mad at myself. That I put you in that position." His fingers run along the steering wheel, not looking at me.

"I hate to tell you this, but I'm an adult. I put myself in that position. And I'd do it again to have Clayton."

"No, I know. I get it. It's just..." He finally looks at me. Will the pain in his eyes ever go away? He has to forgive himself if we're going to move forward. "Gillian..."

"What?"

"Did he touch you?"

I want to chuckle, but I bite my lip to stop. "I got pregnant, Ben."

"No, I mean... you've flinched a couple times when I've gone to touch your face."

I look down, more uncomfortable than I was telling him that Clayton's father is a guy Ben always despised. A guy he got into fights with in the hallways at school. The guy he beat out on the football field. Admitting that the man I chose to sleep with hit me isn't anything I want to relive with Ben.

"Gill..." He tugs me to his side.

I go willingly, wanting the comfort he offers. I suck in a deep breath before I speak. "Twice. Then he left town, and I haven't seen him since."

"Does he know about Clayton?" He wraps his arm around me.

"He knows I was pregnant."

"Did he hit you when you were pregnant?" I don't answer, and he puts his hand under my chin urging it up, so I look at him. "Did he?"

I nod, my chest tight.

He pulls me into him, swallowing me in his warmth and shelter. "I'm gonna kill the bastard."

"He hasn't come back. He's never going to. Who knows, he might have drunk himself to death already," I say.

"Fuck, Gillian, if I hadn't—"

"No, Ben." I slide out of his grip. "No more sorrys. I made a decision, and I've lived with the consequences, one of which is the best thing in my life. It's done and over. He's out of my life forever." I place my hands on his face, forcing him to look at me. "Now kiss me, and if you hit a home run out there, maybe you'll hit a home run later tonight."

I give my best attempt to change this energy in this cab, but the anger hasn't left his stiff body and murderous eyes.

"Don't do that, Gillian."

"It was years ago, and I've made peace with it."

"But you flinched," he says, sounding pained.

"I'm not flinching anymore." I don't even remember flinching. "Come on, Ben."

Someone pounds on the hood of the truck.

"Stop smooching and get your ass out here, Noughton." Brooks laughs and walks toward the field.

"You have to go."

He shakes his head. "I don't have to do anything I don't want to."

"You have to go play. Jude will be pissed."

He holds my gaze. "I don't care about Jude." He pulls me to him again as if he needs to make sure I'm in one piece.

I pull back from him. "Get yourself together, Noughton. Go out there and have fun. I want to sit on the sidelines like I used to and say, 'That's my man.'"

That earns a deep chuckle, even if his eyes are dark.

I slide out of the truck, knowing it's the only way he'll get out.

He finally climbs out and grabs his bag from the back, coming to the front and taking my hand. "I still want to kick his ass."

"If it helps, I kneed him in the balls."

He stops and laughs. "That's my girl."

I love it when he calls me that.

Chapter Twenty-One

BEN

I leave Gillian on the bleachers and head into the dugout, not sure what Jude has planned for me as far as position and where I'll hit in the batting order.

I sit on the bench for a bit, processing what Gillian told me. I can't believe Waylon is Clayton's father. I always hated that fucker. The worst part is, I can't even talk to anyone about it because I would never betray her like that.

"I heard a rumor about you today." Brooks sits next to me.

"Probably not true."

"You bought some lumber for your house?"

I look at Emmett standing at the fence line and flirting with some girl. Snitch.

"Does that mean you're staying?" The same hope is in Brooks's voice that was in Aunt Darla's when she came by this afternoon.

"I can't stand waking up to random women in my kitchen and Emmett taking a shit in my bathroom three times a day."

I don't divulge that I'm thinking about staying for Gillian. I want her to be the first one to know, and it's something we have to talk about. Regardless, I want to be prepared for whatever option we decide on, which means I'm using the summer to build my damn house.

I glance at Brooks and notice he's all decked out with an elbow and ankle guard. I gesture to his protective gear. "Did I miss it when softball turned into an extreme sport?"

"We're playing Wild Bull. They're dirty, and you can never be too careful." He sprawls out, resting his arms on the back of the bench, widening his legs.

"You can't step out of the way of the pitch?"

"Just watch. When I'm taking you to the hospital for a broken elbow, you'll understand. I'll let you borrow my elbow guard after you heal."

"I'll be fine, but thanks."

The rest of our team makes their way into the dugout.

"Okay, line up is..." Jude holds his clipboard in front of him like a general. "Same as always, except I'm sliding Ben into fourth. Sorry, Emmett, you're fifth now."

"Fifth? He comes home, and I get dropped?" Emmett glares at me.

"You had the most strikeouts last season." Jude doesn't even look up to acknowledge Emmett.

"I'm older," I tell my little brother.

"You'll be dropped before the season is over." Emmett puffs out his chest.

"We'll see about that." Nothing like brotherly competition to throw gasoline on the fire crawling through my veins right now. Perfect for me to go out there and hit a home run.

The umpire calls over the captains to start the game.

I grab my mitt from my bag and see Brooks stretching on the field in front of the dugout. "What are you doing?"

"I don't want to pull anything," he says, continuing to twist his body like he's in a yoga class.

"Make sure to stretch your groin, it's probably stiff from lack of use." Lottie puts a wad of bubble gum into her mouth.

"Am I wrong? This is recreational softball?" I ask.

He bends down, and the women on the bleachers whistle at his ass in the air. He blows them a kiss between his legs.

"I feel like I belong over with Wild Bull," I grumble.

Looking across the field, I quickly change my mind. The Wild Bull players look as if they're ready to be drafted into the majors, while we look like a bowling league. This should be fun.

"What's our budget for uniforms?" I ask, nodding to the other team currently taking practice swings in unison.

"Walker Matthews takes this seriously," Brooks says. "He buys all the uniforms, and if you forget an item, you don't play."

I think we need to up our game. Then again, it's fucking recreational softball.

Jude returns after shaking Walker Matthews's hand. "We're home."

Everyone grabs their mitts. Since I already have mine, I step out of the dugout as my cousin Scarlett walks in. She still has her heels on.

"I made it," she says, a little winded.

Romy hands her cleats.

Scarlett handles all the business aspects of the ranch—mostly, I think, all the marketing for the various businesses.

"Where do you want me?" I ask Jude.

"You're going to be a DH."

I frown. "A DH?"

He pats me on the back. "You can cheer for the team."

Great. Since when do softball teams have designated hitters?

Scarlett practices pitching to our cousin Bennett as catcher. At least Jude didn't give me that position. She's all over the plate, and Bennett is dodging left and right to catch the pitches she's throwing.

Walker Matthews heads up to the plate, staring at Scarlett the entire time. "Give me your worst, Scar." He taps his bat on his cleats and takes a few practice swings.

"Go, Scarlett!" the girls cheer, and she gives them a wave.

Scarlett throws her first pitch, and it goes way high. Walker makes a whistling sound as it breezes over his head. She scowls at him. Their dislike for each other is well-known. The constant competition between Wild Bull and Plain Daisy as to who is the bigger and better ranch is endless. When Wild Bull opened up a country store last year, I thought Scarlett was going to lose her mind.

"Purposely walking me, Scar?"

She winces at the nickname and leans forward as if she's a major league pitcher to see what pitch Bennett is signing for between his legs. I'm still struck on how serious they take this game.

Scarlett throws another pitch, and it goes left. Walker steps over the plate and turns toward the fence line, watching the ball hit the fence and bounce back to Bennett.

"Two more, and I'm on first." Walker taps his bat against his cleats again.

Scarlett throws the next pitch, and it hits the ground before bouncing over Bennett's head.

"Come on, Scarlett, you got this!" I peek out of the dugout when I hear Gillian. Her and Laurel clap and cheer after every pitch.

"Maybe get it over the plate this time," Walker says with a shit-eating grin.

It's an unwritten rule between us cousins to not mess with Scarlett. She's always so wound up that we all leave her alone. So I'm not surprised when she scowls at Walker. She throws the last pitch, and it looks good until it veers right, hitting Walker in the hip.

The crowd laughs, and Walker circles his bat like the cocky

fuck he is and jogs to first. "For such a smart businesswoman, you sure have trouble controlling your temper."

"All right, Matthews, enough of the smack talk." Jude steps out of his position as shortstop to calm these two down.

"Try to steal. I dare you." Scarlett straightens her shoulders as Walker's new hire comes up to bat.

He stares at the bleachers a little too long for my liking. His eyes better be on Laurel and not Gillian.

Scarlett throws the first pitch, and the guy sails it past the fence line, scoring two runs. Walker makes a big deal of jumping on the plate as if he swung it and eyes Scarlett on his way back to the dugout.

The next three batters ground out, and I must admit, our infield has some talent. Jude at short. Emmett at third. Lottie at second. Brooks at first. Our pitching could obviously use some work, though.

Walker pitches for his team, and he throws the ball up in the air and catches it as he saunters to the mound. Lottie goes up to the plate first. She hits a fly ball to right field, and the outfielder runs like an Olympic sprinter, catching the ball with a diving catch.

"This team is no joke," I say.

"Told you." Brooks hits his elbow guard before he steps up to the plate.

Brooks grounds out. Jude gets on base with a double, then it's my turn. I put my bat between my legs and run my sweaty hands down my pants.

There are two outs, and if I don't get Jude to home plate, Emmett will for sure stir up shit about me getting placed before him in the batting order. Plus, Gillian is watching me, and I want to show off to her.

"Home run?" I turn and ask her.

She laughs, and Laurel looks at her, wondering what she's missing.

"Triple?"

She shakes her head.

"Home run or nothing?"

She nods. Laurel's forehead scrunches.

Walker throws me a pitch and I think it's a ball, but the umpire says strike.

"Who's paying you?" I grumble.

The second pitch goes to the inside, making me step out of the box, and the umpire calls strike again. I glare at him but don't say anything.

"Boo!" Gillian yells.

"It almost hit him!" Laurel joins in, and I smile.

Walker throws his third pitch, and it's literally a meatball over the plate. I swing and the ball sails toward the outfield. It looks really good, but I run like hell to first and then to second. As I'm about to round second, the entire dugout comes out, and I know I hit a home run.

Jude makes it home and waits for me, his arms open, and pulls me into a hug. The rest of my cousins and Brooks join us, celebrating the tie game.

Emmett grounds out trying to hit the ball too hard to get a home run after me.

It's back and forth, each team not scoring for the next couple of innings. But the smack talk is fierce, and I thought I'd played with some of the worst in the league. They'd be astounded if they came here.

By the time we get to the last inning, Wild Bull is up by one, and it's our last chance to tie or win. Jensen grounds out. Poppy strikes out. There's a reason why she's the ninth hitter. Lottie goes up to the plate, and we're in good shape since we're back to our leadoff hitter.

All the girls in my family have tied their T-shirts in knots at the back, saying they were too big and ruining their game.

Lottie's stomach is exposed, and paired with her shorts, there's a lot of skin showing.

Brooks gets up on deck, taking practice swings. Lottie swivels her ass, and the catcher on Walker's team can't stop staring.

"Hey, eyes on the ball, buddy," Brooks tells him, while his own eyes don't leave Lottie's ass.

Walker throws the pitch, and Lottie swings, fouling the ball off. Brooks is too mesmerized by Lottie's ass, so the ball hits him square in the nuts. He falls to his knees, both hands covering his junk.

Gasps ring out from the bleachers.

A few teammates on both teams snicker while Emmett full out laughs.

"You're telling me you wear all that shit but not a cup?" I shout.

Brooks flips me off, rolling back and forth on the ground.

Lottie goes over to Brooks and squats. She whispers something in his ear, and Brooks grunts and groans.

Brooks waddles into the dugout and Jude tosses him an ice pack from a cooler.

"Pinch hitter," Jude calls. "Scarlett, you're at bat."

She looks up from her phone, her shoulders sinking. "I hate batting."

"Well, we have no choice."

She puts her phone down and grabs a helmet and a bat.

"She's not good," Jude whispers to me.

"I heard you!" Scarlett glares over her shoulder, but she doesn't take any practice swings. She doesn't even watch the pitches coming in.

Lottie shoots a ball right over the shortstop's head. The left fielder can't get there fast enough, so she reaches first base.

She jumps up and down on the base. "Come on, Scarlett! You got this!"

"Fucking Christ." Brooks grabs his junk again.

I bite down on my lip. I'm fairly sure Brooks likes Lottie, and the way she's jumping and things are bouncing it looks like pure torture for him.

Scarlett goes up to the plate. Walker throws the first pitch and it's perfect, but Scarlett swings and misses.

We all shout words of encouragement to her.

She nods and narrows her eyes at Walker.

"I'll give you a real easy one," he baits her, then throws another perfect pitch down the middle.

She swings and misses.

"You got this!" Gillian screams.

"Hit it right back at him!" Laurel yells.

"Last one, Scar." Walker exaggerates all his movements, and the third ball comes in perfect position for a hit.

"Swing!" Jude screams right when she should.

Scarlett does, and the ball flies. Lottie runs, and being the track star she was, she's practically at third before Scarlett reaches first.

The ball hits the top of the fence and falls over.

"Home run!" we scream and run out to home plate.

All nine of us jump up and down with our arms around each other. While I've been away, I forgot what it was like to be with all my cousins. The way we all have one another's backs and how we're each other's biggest cheerleaders.

Wild Bull sulks off the field with their bags.

I wink at Gillian before I go back into the dugout to grab my bag.

It's good to be home.

Chapter Twenty-Two

GILLIAN

Friday night comes, and I purposely wear another sundress. For Ben, and also because it's hot as hell outside.

Clayton comes out of his bedroom, his phone in his hand, a bag swung over his shoulder.

"Ready for Drew's?" I ask.

His eyes lift, and he stares at the dress. "Going out with the boyfriend?"

"Coach Noughton? Yeah."

He nods and goes to watch out the window for Betsy to pick him up.

"Hey, Clay. How would you feel if I had Ben over for dinner?"

His chest rises and falls with a sigh. "You know how much shit I'm getting."

"Language."

"Sorry," he mumbles. "The other kids think Coach Reyes favors me because he wants to be on Coach Noughton's favorite list."

"I get it, I do, but you're a talented player. Coach Reyes sees that. Even Ben said the other day how good you are."

"He did?" His eyes widen.

"Yeah. Asked who you've been working with."

"Did you tell him?"

I don't mention that the conversation took another turn. A turn toward his dad and all the shit I never want Clayton to know. It's bad enough his dad left the minute he found out I was pregnant. I don't need to tell him that his dad physically abused me too. "I didn't."

"Why not?"

"I will. We got sidetracked."

He screws up his face. "Ew."

I give him a pointed stare. "Not like that."

He glances out the window, then turns to me, his phone never leaving his hands. "I never understood why he helped me, but I get it now."

"What do you get?"

"He did it because of Coach Noughton. To make amends for him leaving you."

I sigh. "Maybe partly, but I think he just wanted to help you. Probably saw the raw talent that everyone else sees. But don't go getting a big head."

I walk across the room and ruffle his hair. He ducks and moves away as Betsy pulls up in the driveway and honks the horn.

"Gotta go." He kisses my cheek. "Bye, Mom."

"Bye. Be careful."

He turns with his hand on the doorknob. "You too." He smirks.

"Go!" I shake my head.

He laughs and walks out to the truck, getting in the back of Betsy's big Suburban. I wave from the window. I catch Ben waiting for Betsy to pull out of the driveway so he can pull in, and I grab my purse.

This giddy feeling bubbling in my stomach is bad news. Bad news because I'm becoming more and more attached, and there's still a small part of me that can't stop worrying about what the future will bring.

I open the door as Ben's climbing out of his truck. "I was coming to get you."

"Well, here I am."

He thumbs toward the street, though Betsy is gone. "Was that Clayton?"

I nod and lock up, walking toward him.

He shuts his door and meets me at the front of his truck. When Ben takes me into his arms, his lips find mine. My arms wind around his neck, and my fingers play with his hair. I close my eyes, relishing the moment.

He ends the kiss, and I whimper. Drawing back, he holds me while looking down between us. "You look amazing."

"Thanks." I step away and twirl. "Sundress."

"You know I love them."

"I do." Heat runs through my body, and I'm sure I'm blushing from his attention.

"Let's go. I have big plans for us."

"I can't wait."

He follows me to the passenger side of his truck and opens the door. I step into the doorway, rise on my tiptoes, and give him a kiss before climbing in.

After climbing into the cab, he starts the truck and soaks me in again. Then he shakes his head with a smile so wide I want to ask what he's thinking, but I don't need the words. I think he's just as happy as I am.

❧

Ben drives toward Plain Daisy Ranch, bypassing his family home and going down the small road that circles the lake where most of the family homes are located.

"Where are we going?" I ask, having only been in this area once or twice over the years.

"I should have blindfolded you."

"Oh, I like where this is going." I waggle my eyebrows.

He shakes his head and laughs, pulling down a track that's just two tire marks through a line of trees.

A clearing comes into view, and I smile, seeing the stacks of lumber on the ground. I turn to look at him, but he doesn't react, instead parking next to the area where I assume he'll be building his house.

Laurel told me at the softball game that rumors were spreading about the two of us and that everyone thinks that Ben buying lumber means he'll be sticking around. But I didn't want to ask him and put him on the spot. I figured he'd share when he wanted to, and now I think he is.

He puts the truck in park and looks at me. "As you probably guessed, this is my house that's going to be built."

I step out of the truck, and he meets me by the stacks of wood. "Sick of waking up to your dad and his dates?"

He wraps his arms around my waist, resting his chin on my head. "Part of it, but"—his hands land on my hips and he turns me to face him—"I want a permanent place here."

I smile. I've waited a long time for him to say he wants to stay in Willowbrook, but now I'm at a loss for words.

"Before you say anything, I know you have the bar exam results coming, and you said before that you wanted to interview in big cities. That you wanted to leave Willowbrook."

I don't tell him I'm questioning all that now. "I—"

"I'm not asking you to give up any of that. I just want you to know that I want us. I want a future together, and me building this house hopefully helps you trust that I'm not going anywhere. I'm right where I want to be."

I step away from him, and his hands fall to his sides. Turning away to gather my thoughts, I stare at the lumber. This is everything I've ever wanted to hear from him. But a part of me is still afraid something better will come along—a job, an opportunity, something.

"What about the football analyst job?"

"I can do that from anywhere. Fly in and out. But, as crazy as it sounds, I'm really enjoying coaching. So much is up in the air with Coach Marks. He's doing well, but he brought up retirement to me last week. I got to thinking..."

"Are you telling me you want to stay in Willowbrook and coach football?"

He shrugs. "I'm saying I enjoy coaching way more than I thought I would." He steps up to me and takes my hand, pulling me in. "Talk to me. What are you thinking?"

"I'm thinking it's a pretty big change in your way of thinking. I'm wondering if I went to law school for nothing. I'm thinking how much I love everything you're saying."

His cocky grin emerges. "First of all, it is a change, but it's always been you. I lost my way once, and I'll never do it again. Second, you didn't go to law school for nothing. I can find a coaching position wherever you land. Third, I love you."

"Oh, Ben." I sigh, unable to process those three words falling from his mouth.

"I went out and lived my dream of becoming a pro. But I never felt fulfilled. It was because of you. So much of me was still in Willowbrook with you. You're my future. Location doesn't matter as long as I'm with you. If this house has to be where we stay when we visit my family, so be it."

Unable to say anything, I push up on my toes and kiss him. He grips my waist and tugs me to him, deepening the kiss. It's not until he pulls back and his thumb runs along my cheek that I realize I'm crying.

"This is a good thing." He laughs, brushing away more tears.

"I know. It is. But we have an uphill battle. We have Clayton, for one. Plus, I mean, you just got back. I don't want to be the reason you leave. Your family..."

I know how happy they are to have him back.

"And we'll deal with it all. Together. But tonight..." He takes my hand and leads me down a path past where his house will be built.

I hear the trickling of water before we arrive at the river's edge.

"Ben."

He smiles.

He re-created the scene from our last night together. The pillows. The blankets. The tealights sprinkled around.

He turns to me and takes my hands. "I want a do-over. I know we can't rewind time, and we wouldn't want to anyway. You wouldn't have Clayton, and we were two naive kids the last time we were here. But I feel it, Gillian. This is our time. I want to put the past behind us and look toward the future, starting tonight."

My chest feels as if it might burst from happiness. More tears stream down my face, and I use my palm to wipe them away. "Jeez."

"I wasn't looking to make you cry."

I chuckle, batting more away. "I know. I just... I love you so much."

He rushes to me, wrapping an arm around my waist and his lips falling to mine. Our tongues tangle, and I climb up his body, his hands finding my ass.

"God, I love you." He casts small kisses along my neck.

"Me too." I can't get close enough to him. "I need you."

He chuckles, walking us somewhere, but I'm too busy kissing every inch of his face and neck. He lowers my feet to the ground, his hands resting on my hips, and stares down at me before he brushes my neck and shoulders with kisses. Shivers run up my spine, and a moan slips out of me.

He reaches around me, his fingers manipulating the zipper of my dress. His hands crawl up my back, taking the sleeves of my dress down each arm, one at a time. "I've wanted to see this dress on the ground since I picked you up."

The dress drops around my feet, revealing my pale pink bra and matching underwear. His fingers unclasp my bra, and the lacy fabric joins my dress.

He continues to kiss my collarbone, his lips trailing down my body before stopping at my breasts. He cups one in his palm while his mouth takes the other one. His tongue flicks the nipple of one while his thumb runs circles with the other.

I'm in sensory overload. It's been too long.

"You're perfection," he whispers. He leaves my breasts too soon and falls to his knees, his hands resting on my hips, pulling me to him. He runs his knuckles down the front of my silk thong, and I gasp. "So wet. So ready for me."

Reaching down, he takes off my shoes one at a time, and my feet land on the soft blankets he's laid out.

"Lie down for me."

I get down on the plush surface, laying my head on the pillows.

He slips off his shoes but remains dressed.

"What about you?" I ask.

"Not yet." I whimper as Ben's hands slide up my legs, inching toward my center. He pushes my panties aside and runs a finger along my slickness. "I've missed this. How wet you get for me."

My back arches from his touch. When he lies down, his lips run up my thighs. He hooks his fingers into the sides of my thong, and I inch off the blanket, allowing him to slip the fabric down my legs.

He nestles between my thighs, first inhaling, then he plays with me using his fingers. I was already on the brink of an orgasm, and when he buries his fingers inside me, I cry out. My hands fall to my sides, clenching the blanket. I rock against his hand, and he sucks my clit into his hot mouth, his tongue circling the nub and setting off a magnitude of sensations that bring me right to the cusp.

He adds another finger, and I meet the push of his fingers with the thrust of my hips.

"I'm going to come," I pant, a wave of pleasure overtaking my body.

Ben doesn't relent, his fingers wrecking me until I'm a tight ball of blissed-out mess. His teeth graze my clit, and I tip over the edge he so expertly brought me to.

My entire body bolts off the blanket, my hands reaching for him. I say his name again, but this time my tone is soft and loving. I've missed him so much.

He slides up my body, leaving a path of wetness from his kisses until he's completely over me. His lips take mine, and I taste myself on his tongue.

"You have too many clothes." I grasp at his shirt, and he reaches back, tearing it off his body. "I need you inside me."

His lips leave my skin, and he sits up and unbuckles his pants, then stands to shed both his pants and boxer briefs down his legs, giving me a gorgeous view of his naked body with the trees as a backdrop.

I move to my knees, but Ben shakes his head and lowers his body over mine. His dick runs along my opening as he reaches under the pillow, pulling out a condom. Needing more, desperately seeking friction, I circle my hips, and he growls.

"You do that, and Clayton's going to have a baby brother or sister," he says, sitting up on his knees.

I rise to my elbows, watching him slide the condom down his length.

Then he's over me again and plunges into me, sinking in fully while a strangled sound rushes out of his lungs. "Fuck, Gill. How did I ever go this long without you?"

I grab the back of his head and pull him down to me. Our tongues tangle, and our bodies rock together. He rises on his elbows, staring at me, and tears prick my eyes from the elated glow in his soft brown irises. No one ever made me feel so safe, so cared for, so connected.

I wrap my legs around his waist, and he pumps harder. I lose myself in his crazed, lustful look, and my fingers claw at his back, another orgasm on the brink.

"Harder," I say, desperate to get back to the ecstasy only he can give me.

His hips move faster, and our bodies slide together from the sweat between us. The sound of my wetness echoes through the tree-filled area, overtaking the sound of the running river.

My lower body rises off the blankets, meeting his thrusts, and I come so hard, it's like a meteor shower behind my closed eyelids.

Ben stills and jerks inside me a couple of times before collapsing on me, his warm breath tracing my neck. He kisses my neck and lifts his head, one hand smoothing the hair stuck to my forehead. "I forgot how fucking hot you are when you come."

I pull him back down to me, kissing him and hoping he feels every bit inside of me that he's touched. It's game over for us. There's no turning back now. I'm on the road to happily ever after—or heartbreak.

Chapter Twenty-Three

BEN

Gillian is not in bed when I wake up, so I get up and dress just in case. Clayton was supposed to spend the night at Drew's, but after the last time, I can't be too careful.

I open her bedroom door, and the smell of bacon makes my stomach growl.

Gillian's in front of the stove in a cute matching silk shorts and tank pajama set. "Have a good sleep?"

"Why are you up so early? I had hopes of waking you." I bear hug her from behind and kiss the nape of her neck. I'm never going to get enough of her. I'm ready to wake up to her every morning.

"After you have kids, you just become an early riser. Maybe once he's in college, I'll find the luxury of sleeping in again." She threads her fingers through my hair, holding my face to her neck. I kiss her again, and she releases me.

This is probably a good time to bring up something I've been wondering about. "Question about that..."

I hold my hand out for the tongs, and she willingly gives them to me, but goes to the fridge and pulls out eggs.

"Question about what?"

"Do you want more kids? I mean..." She's enough for me, but I wouldn't mind little Gillians and Bens running around.

She cracks a few eggs into a bowl and throws away the shells, not answering me at first. I'm guessing the answer is no, but Gillian is a thinker. Rarely does she talk about something serious without making sure she's thought it through.

"Is that a no?" I finally ask.

She shakes her head and scrambles the eggs. "No, but my pregnancy with Clayton wasn't easy." She pours the eggs into another pan. "I made peace a long time ago with Clayton being an only child, but—"

I put down the tongs and slide my finger into the waistband of her shorts, pulling her toward me. "It's okay. It's not a game-changer for me."

She looks up at me with a sweet smile. "I was going to say... but now I realize there's an opportunity, and I've always wanted to have your children." I grin, and she rolls her eyes. "Don't look so arrogant."

"I'm just saying I wouldn't mind impregnating you."

"Oh my god, could you make it sound more medical?"

I pull her even closer, and her head tilts back. I hover inches from her face. "How about, I want nothing more than to fuck you every minute of every day so I can fill you with my seed?"

She screws up her face. "Yeah. Not doing it for me."

"Okay, I've got it.... I want you to see your belly swollen with our child."

She shrugs, but her smile grows.

"I want to suffer through midnight feedings and diaper explosions with you."

She cringes. "I'm not sure you understand what you're saying."

"I want to make Clayton a big brother because I know he'll be a great one."

She grins. "Bingo! You win, Ben Noughton."

My lips fall to hers, and I find myself not wanting to pull away but knowing I have to.

"But we have a lot of steps before any of that happens," she says.

I turn the bacon over, not responding because I don't mind speeding down the fast lane when it comes to Gillian. We can hit those steps one, two, three.

We finish making breakfast and sit down at her table for four.

"Coach Reyes loves Clayton," I say, stabbing my eggs.

"He told me that."

"He's really good, Gill. Who did you say helped him out?"

"I didn't." She snaps a piece of bacon and eats it.

I frown. "Do you not want to tell me?"

She sits back in her chair, lifting her coffee to her lips. "No. I mean, it's not a big deal."

"You're being vague." I can't imagine it being anyone I would care about. "I'm just curious because his hands are really good. And the way he reads the ball."

Her shoulders sink, and she inhales a deeper breath, letting it go. "It was mostly one person, but a few others helped."

I shake my head at how uncomfortable she is to tell me. He's not my son. I'm not territorial about it. I can wait until she wants to tell me.

"Your dad. Jude and Emmett helped too."

The air squeezes from my lungs, and my gaze falls to my full plate. "My dad?"

"You know how peewee football is around here. Your dad came to one of the games. I tried to help Clay, I did. But he was struggling. Barely getting time off the bench. This town is so damn serious about their football." Her eyes well up, but she swallows it down. "I tried to get him to focus on a different sport, but football was always his favorite. Koa was never into football, and my dad was always working. I watched videos, but honestly, I just didn't know how to help make him better. One day, your dad asked if I would mind, that he didn't want to step on my toes, and I said yes."

"My dad?" I ask again. I just never thought it would be him.

She sips her coffee and places the mug on the table. "I think he thought... well..."

"He was doing it because his son left you." My chest aches, and I rub it with my palm.

She shrugs. "I'm not sure. He never said that. Maybe he was just doing it to be nice. Help the underdog kind of thing."

My dad is a great guy. It's probably a combination of both.

"And Jude and Emmett?"

"They'd help when it came to running drills. We'd go over there on Sundays, and they'd work while I cooked dinner as a thanks to them for helping Clayton."

I push away my plate. "They never said anything."

"Are you mad?" She bites her bottom lip.

I turn my attention to her. Am I? No. It's just another thing to feel fucking guilty about, but I'm not putting my issues on Gillian. She wants us to move forward, and I do too. That doesn't mean the guilt will ever leave me.

I shake my head. "I'm glad he got the help he needed. And I hate to admit it, but they did a great job. His fundamentals are unmatched out there on the field."

"I'm sorry I hadn't told you. I know you probably feel like it should've been you, or maybe you don't, I don't know."

It's so weird to be with someone who knows me so well. I can't believe I ever gave this up.

"Come here." I slide my chair back. She walks over and climbs into my lap. I run my hand up her back, cradling the back of her head, my fingers tangling in her dark strands. "Never be afraid to tell me anything. I'm a big boy. And I just want you to know that once Clayton is okay with us, I'm taking over."

She runs her hand down my stubbled face. "Okay."

I pull her down to my face, and our lips are about to touch when the front door opens.

"You've got to be kidding me!"

Clayton's home.

 ❧

I PULL INTO THE DRIVEWAY AT MY FAMILY'S HOME. It's Saturday, so my dad and brothers are likely down in the ranch area. After Clayton got home, he went to his room, Gillian and I ate breakfast, and I left. This whole trying to let Clayton come to terms with us isn't helping us move forward.

I walk down to the cattle area, and Bessie, our Guernsey cow, is at the fence line. She was just a calf when I left for college, and she's our oldest cow. It's a miracle she's still alive. I think my brothers and I all love her so much because she's such a great mother to her calves. If I thought too long about it, I could probably make some correlation to us growing up without a mother, but why bother?

Jude spots me and rides up on Titan, his horse. "What brings you down here?"

I run my hand down Titan's nose. "I came to see Dad, but I have a question for you too."

He climbs off Titan and walks with him toward the horse barn. "What's up?"

"Why didn't anyone tell me you guys helped Clayton when he was younger? Trained with him so he'd get some playing time."

He grunts. "Gillian told you, huh?"

"Yeah. Why the secret?"

We walk into the horse barn, and he brings Titan into his stall. "Why does it matter? He's not yours."

"But Gillian..."

He laughs. "What? Is yours? You sticking around then?"

My blood boils, at my limit for all the shit he gives me for leaving. "What the hell is wrong with you? You want me to apologize?"

He shuts the door to the stable. "I don't want your apologies."

I follow him as he walks out of the barn.

Emmett arrives on Brutus, climbing off while the horse is still prancing. He's such a moron sometimes. "Hold up. Let me get some popcorn."

"Fuck off, Emmett," I say, continuing after Jude. "Just come at me. Get it out of your system."

Jude turns around. "It's nothing. Your skin too thin to take a joke now?"

"You're not joking. You're making digs. I'm sorry, okay? I'm sorry for leaving to go pursue my dream and that you didn't get to. I get that you were left to take care of the ranch. There's nothing I can do about that."

"You're fucking clueless." Jude steps up to me, our chests almost brushing.

"Hey." Emmett comes between us and puts his hand on each of our chests. "You're brothers."

"Shut up, Emmett," we say in unison.

We stare one another down, me an inch taller, which doesn't make any difference. It'd be a fair fight.

"It's not that you left, Ben. But think about the shape of the ranch when you left. Think about how it was failing. We did need you here, but I told Dad to let you go. That I'd manage it, that Emmett could do more."

I look at Emmett, and he nods with a frown. Not that I don't believe my big brother.

"Why didn't anyone tell me?"

"You were a little lost in Gilly Be's world." Emmett shrugs.

"You wouldn't have gone had we told you. I'm fucking proud of you," Jude says. "You did it. You made it. But when you made it, you turned your back on your family. How many holidays went by that you didn't come home? You sent a fucking shipment of gifts one year. We didn't want the expensive shit, we wanted you. Didn't realize that when we sent you off into the world, you'd hardly ever come back."

I don't have a response. I did rarely come home, but it had more to do with not wanting to run into Gillian. And if I'm being really truthful, I didn't want to feel the guilt that usually accompanied returning home.

"Fuck." I tug at my hair, stepping back from my brothers.

"What's going on here?" My dad walks Legend over to us by his reins.

Obviously all three of them were out doing something, and it makes it clear how much time they spend together.

"Nothing." Jude turns his back to walk away, but my dad puts his hand on Jude's chest.

"It doesn't look like nothing." He eyes me, but I don't say anything. Dad shifts his attention to Emmett because everyone knows he'll fold.

"The boiled water just spilled over the pot," Emmett says.

I roll my eyes.

My dad nods. "Family meeting."

Jude's head rocks back and rolls to the side. "I have shit to do."

"I tell you the shit you have to do. Let's go."

Jude goes back and grabs Titan out of his stall, Emmett gets back on Brutus, and I take Magnum. After we saddle them, Dad leads the way on Legend. We follow, and my ass instantly hurts since I'm not used to riding anymore. I've only ridden a couple times since I've been back.

Our horses climb the path up the small hill covered in a plethora of daisies. Up on top are the tombstones of generations before us. We secure our horses to the tree, and my dad approaches my mom's grave while the three of us stay back to give him space.

"Boys are at it again, Daisy, but I'm sure you saw it comin'." He kisses his fingers and touches the top of the tombstone.

Jude goes next because everything goes by birth order in our family. "Ben's being an asshole, Ma." Jude smiles back at me, then kisses his fingers and touches the top of her tombstone.

I approach, mad at myself that I haven't come up here since returning. *Daisy Noughton, loving wife and mother* is etched in the gray stone.

"Jude's been keeping secrets." I kiss the tips of my fingers and press them to the sun-warmed stone.

We stand to the side as Emmett approaches for this turn. "They're all crazy. I'm the only sane one." He bends down and kisses the tombstone with his lips.

Dad shakes his head. "Now, Jude, what the hell is going on?"

"Why does Jude always get to go first?" I ask, hands on my hips.

"He's the oldest."

I blow out a breath.

"He's up my ass about me joking about him not being around. Oh, and the fact that Gillian told him we helped Clayton."

My dad looks at me.

"The Clayton thing wasn't why we were fighting," I say.

"I want this all behind us now," my dad says.

Emmett sits on the grass since he's not part of it.

"I told him that he should've come home more often," Jude says.

Dad blows out a breath. "I'm pretty sure he regrets that he didn't. Don't you, Ben?"

"Yeah. I just... damn it. When is the guilt going to stop?" I let a frustrated groan slip past my lips.

"What do you feel guilty about?" Dad asks, and Jude scoffs.

"Everything. Leaving you guys. Getting out of this town. The money in my bank account. My fame. Gillian. Her...'" I stop myself before I mention her getting hit by some douchebag. "You guys helping Clayton when it should've been me. I love being back here, but the guilt just keeps piling on." I look at Jude. "I'm sorry for not coming home enough, but it was easier staying away."

"You can't bury things. It all comes out eventually. And that goes for feelings too." Dad looks at Jude. "Your turn."

Jude throws up his hands. "I'm proud of your accomplishments, Ben. You worked your ass off to get where you did. I love working the ranch. You might not, and maybe that's why you think it's some chore for me. But it's not like that. I love my life."

"You mean you love Sadie," Emmett chimes in, laughing until our dad cuts him a look. "Sorry."

"My problem was you not coming home and acting like sending your money replaced you. We lost Mom, and I felt like we lost you too."

I take in what he's saying.

"Ben, you have to make peace with your past, otherwise you'll never have a future. It seems like you and Gillian are making another go at it, and you're building the house. Everybody would like to rewind time and have a do-over. But you need to face what's in front of you now. You obviously feel an immense amount of guilt about the past. But we're your family. We will always forgive you." Dad looks at Jude, and Jude nods. "You bury all that shit here and now. And then you try to be a better man."

"You make it sound so easy." I kick the grass with my boot.

"It's not, but you have to try. From an outsider's perspective, I gotta tell you, you're just wallowing in the past."

I nod, knowing my dad is right. "I'm sorry for not coming home more."

"I'm sorry for the digs," Jude replies.

"I'm sorry for being the hottest Noughton." Emmett laughs.

Dad shakes his head. "Group hug."

We all circle around Mom's tombstone, linking our arms over each other's shoulders, and stare down at her grave.

"Love you," we say in unison.

We climb back on our horses and head to the stables, all of us lost in our thoughts. I can't speak for them, but I always try to remember as many things about my mom as I can whenever we leave her gravesite. Somehow, having the Jude thing behind me, the pressure in my chest loosens a bit.

Chapter Twenty-Four

GILLIAN

Laurel is working on another elaborate wedding cake when I arrive at the bakery.

"Look who came back to the world of the living." She eyes me over the buttercream.

"Sorry. I know. I've been a bad friend." I sit on the stool across from her.

"You're not being a bad friend. You're in the bliss stage. When you can't get enough of each other. I'm perfectly fine taking a back seat."

"Thanks for understanding. It's crazy, right? I'm crazy."

She puts the piping bag down and places her palms on the table. "No. You're not crazy. You're in love. And love makes you crazy." She shrugs. "So maybe a little crazy, but not the crazy you're talking about." We both laugh, and she picks up her piping bag. "I'm proud of you. You're not harping on the future. You're living in the moment. Feels good, right?"

I shrug. "Clayton still doesn't want to have dinner with him."

She inhales and switches her piping back to a silvery gray.

This cake is going to be beautiful. "I know you hate it, but you might have to just tell him he has to."

I sigh. "I know. I just... everything is going so well."

"Is it?" I feel her judgment whether she means for me to or not.

"You're the one who told me not to worry about the future."

"Is Clayton a kid you still have in the future?"

"Laurel." I groan, understanding what she's saying. "I can feel that Ben wants to get that ball rolling too."

"Clayton wants to protect you, and probably himself too. His deadbeat dad abandoned him before he was even born. Although Clayton never met him, it must hurt. Ben left you once before, so he wants to protect you from that happening again. But at some point, Clayton has to see that Ben makes you happy, that you've forgiven Ben, and that Ben feels remorse for what happened. That's what Clayton needs to move forward."

I nod, agreeing with everything she says.

"He's a good kid. You raised him well. Would you rather have a kid who didn't care? He just needs a little kick in the ass. And then you can be one big happy family."

I think back to my conversation with Ben. "He asked me if I wanted more kids."

She gives me one of her swoony smiles. "And?"

"I told him yeah."

"Are you going to wait to tell Clayton until you're in labor with his new baby brother or sister?"

I pick up an icing tool and toss it at her. It falls to the floor.

"Now you have to wash it," she says.

Rounding the table, I pick it up and go over to the sink.

"And the bar exam?" This is Laurel. Miss Don't Think About the Future, but...

"The results haven't come in yet, but I'm not sure what

my plan is." I dry the utensil and put it back on the tray before sitting on the stool, watching her work. I'm amazed by my best friend's craftsmanship. "Ben said he'd move anywhere I want to go."

The icing bag slips from her hand, but she grabs it before it falls to the table. "Seriously?"

I nod.

"That's a good thing."

"It is."

She studies me for a second. "Then why don't you look happy?"

"I don't want to take him away from his family again. I'm not even sure I want to leave now. I mean, everything, other than the Clayton thing, is going so great. Ben's enjoying coaching. He said he could find another coaching job, but can he? I think there's something special about him coaching the Wildcats."

Laurel puts down the icing bag and sits on the stool next to me. "You love Ben. So, you want him to be happy."

I nod.

"But he already lived his dream, Gill. He went off and got to be a professional football player. Maybe Ben's dream now is just to have you in his life. This is your chance. Your chance to make your dream come true."

I understand what she's saying. "I love Ben. I love Clayton. I love Bruce, Jude, and Emmett. I love everyone in town. Bruce helped me when I had no one to turn to when it came to Clayton. How do I take his son from him after he just got him back?"

She nods, understanding my predicament. "I don't want you to sacrifice any more. You worked hard to get your law degree, and believe me, I want you here, but what I want is for you to make your dream come true." She squeezes my hand, rises, and goes to the other side of the table to finish her cake.

The bell rings, and I head out into the shop to help the customer.

As always, Laurel has given me a lot to think about.

§⁊

I'M LYING IN BED WHEN A TEXT MESSAGE POPS UP ON my phone.

> Want to go for a drive?

> It's eleven-thirty and Clayton's asleep.

> Just come outside. Trust me.

I throw the covers off and get out of bed, peeking out the window. Ben's truck is there, but he's not in it. And there's a sheriff's car. What the hell is going on?

Sliding into my flip-flops, I open the door. Ben's all smiles in shorts and a new Willowbrook Wildcats T-shirt.

"Hey, Gillian," Brooks says next to Ben.

He's dressed in shorts, no shirt with his Sheriff vest. "Brooks." I nod.

He blows out a breath, staring blankly at me.

"Brooks will sit in the house in case Clayton wakes up," Ben says.

"You will?" I ask Brooks.

"Apparently." He rolls his eyes.

"I got you a coffee and a dozen donuts." Ben shoves them into his chest.

"You're an asshole." He cradles the coffee and opens the box. His eyes light up. "Oh, Boston cream."

"Ready?" Ben asks, ignoring his poor friend who has to sit on my couch while I go make out with Ben somewhere.

"I feel bad," I say.

Ben takes my hand. "He's fine. Right, Brooks?"

"What if he wakes up?" Brooks looks downright frightened by the thought.

"He's not an infant," Ben says.

"He's a heavy sleeper," I assure him and let Ben pull me away.

Brooks steps in and looks around space as if he's conducting a raid.

I climb into the cab of Ben's truck and slide next to him, wanting to be close. I kiss the side of his neck, and he wraps his arm around me, pulling me even closer. I am so head over heels for this man.

We drive through town, and he takes me to the spot he took me for breakfast. The moon shines down on the hills, reflecting off the small lake. He backs up, and we go around to the truck bed, laying a blanket down in it.

Being eager, I climb up and lie down before him. He bends down, kisses me, and falls to his back, tucking his arm along my side as I curl into him. The sky is clear, filled with a million stars.

"It's beautiful," I say.

"Yeah."

I slide my cheek along his chest and look up at him, our eyes meeting. "I love you."

"I love you." His fingers graze my arm, causing shivers in the warm night air. "Gill?"

The tone he's using is the same as when he told me he was going to Clemson. My body stiffens, and he runs his fingers down my arm again.

"What is it?" I say, unable to meet his eyes.

"I want to have a relationship with Clayton."

The tension leaves my body. "Okay."

"I know we agreed to take our time, but I feel like we're in limbo until he accepts me as a part of your life."

I swing one leg over and lie on top of him. Our breaths mingle, and he runs his hands down my hair, twirling it with his finger.

"You're right. We need to make it happen. I'll set it up."

I kiss him, and he winds my hair around his hand, deepening the kiss. His other hand slides under the back of my tank top, running along the small of my back, making the hunger that always sits under the surface rise to the forefront.

I lift the hem of his shirt and run my hands up his bare chest. "So many muscles."

He links his hands behind his head, watching me intently. "The moonlight looks beautiful on you."

He watches me explore his body, and I slide my finger down to the sprinkle of hair that runs from his navel, disappearing under the waist of his shorts. My gaze remains on him as I slide his shorts down over his hardened cock.

"No boxer briefs?" I tilt my head, and he chuckles.

I palm his length, and it throbs in my hand, pulsating as if begging me to play with it. I scoot down his legs and lean forward. He rises on his elbows, intent on watching me.

"Gillian," he practically groans.

My tongue runs up his length, and his head rocks back but bounces back up to see what I do next. I grip the base and wrap my lips around his cock.

He rasps a breath. "Fuck." He falls to his back but gets on his elbows again. "I love watching you with my cock in your mouth."

I twirl my tongue around the tip, then sink deeper, so the tip of his dick hits the back of my throat. His cock twitches. I suck him coming back up, twisting my hand around his thickness.

I used to know exactly how Ben liked it, and I hate that a part of me is self-conscious that I may not know what he loves now. But his reactions tell me he's loving what I'm doing, so I continue.

"Shit. It feels so damn good."

I peek up at him, and he leverages himself to put one hand on my head, his thumb running along my cheek. Our eyes lock, and I pump him as he slides his thumb into my mouth. I suck it into my mouth, keeping my gaze on him. He shakes his head as if in disbelief that this is happening.

He pulls his thumb out, and I go back to his dick, working him over and over, doing every move that pulls a grunt, growl, or groan out of him. His hips thrust, and I smile around his length, knowing he's about to come. I love being the one responsible for him losing control.

"I'm coming," he warns, but I don't move away. He pushes into my mouth, coming so hard a strangled sound erupts out of him. "FUUCCKK!"

I lick him clean, giving the head of his cock one more kiss before tucking him back into his shorts and crawling up his body.

"Damn, Gill."

I kiss him, and his hand glides down the back of my shorts.

"What are you doing?" I ask.

He rolls me over to my back and straddles my thighs, his fingers hooking into the waistband of my shorts. "It's my turn to see if you're going commando."

"Spoiler. I'm not."

His eyes turn ravenous.

An hour later, we leave the serene view of the moonlight over the rolling Nebraska hills and head back to Willowbrook.

Not wanting to leave him, I snuggle up to him in the cab of the truck. "I don't want to say goodbye."

"Me either."

Ultimately, we have no choice, so when he parks at my

house, Ben opens his door, and I go out his side instead of the passenger side. He holds my hand on the walk up to the porch, and I press the keycode into the lock.

"Welcome home." Clayton sits on the chair with the remote in his hand.

Brooks is on the couch, fast asleep, with a half-eaten donut rising and falling on his chest.

"Nice babysitter you got me." He stands and saunters down the hallway.

"Baby steps," I say to Ben.

But we need to be taking big steps. I'm going to have to put on my big girl panties and talk to my son, no matter how much he doesn't want to.

Chapter Twenty-Five

BEN

My phone rings with an unknown number. I slide my thumb, answering it. "Hello?"

"Ben Noughton?"

My hand clenches the phone at the sound of a female voice. I haven't changed my number since coming home, and there are a certain number of women in San Francisco who may still have it. I would never want Gillian thinking I'm talking to them. "This is he."

"My name is Blythe Chen. I'm with *Sportsverse*. We heard that you were coaching a football team in your hometown now."

I look at the field where all the players are currently doing their drills. "I am. Filling in for my previous coach."

"We'd love to do a piece on you. We actually have cameras already at the University of Nebraska for a story and would love to send them down to film a short piece on you this week."

"This week?" How the hell am I supposed to prepare for this week?

"We understand it's short notice, but we're doing something fun with some of the players who have retired recently. Sort of a 'what are they doing now?' thing."

"Okay..."

"We're not going to do anything in-depth. Don't worry." She laughs. "So, are you in?"

It would be a great way for me to get this town some notoriety and hopefully boost tourism. Kind of repaying them for getting me where I got. "Sure."

"Great. Let me get all the dates and times sorted and I'll call you back. We appreciate the opportunity."

"Yeah. No problem."

She hangs up, and I pocket my phone.

"Coach Reyes. Coach Smith." I call them over because we're going to have to get our shit together to look good for this thing. "*Sportsverse* is coming down this week to do a piece on us."

"What?" Coach Reyes's eyes light up. This is clearly a dream for him.

"It's a small piece, kind of like, 'is Ben Noughton sitting on his ass after retirement? Oh no, he's coaching high school football.'"

"Cool." Coach Smith nods, apparently uncaring either way.

"She'll get back to me on a date. I'm not sure how extensive it will be, but we need to be prepared."

Coach Reyes runs his hands over his hair. "I should get a haircut."

Coach Smith stares at him and sighs.

"I'll let you know the details as I get them."

Coach Reyes talks to Coach Smith as they walk away about whether there will be makeup people.

I pull my phone from my pocket and shoot Gillian a text.

Sportsverse is going to do a piece on me coaching the Wildcats.

The three dots appear immediately.

That's awesome! Are you excited?

The truth is, not really. I was just getting to a good place with the boys and having them see me as Coach Noughton and not Ben Noughton, former San Francisco wide receiver.

I'm not sure. But it's good for Willowbrook.

For sure. Congratulations!

Hey. Bar exam results?

Heard a rumor maybe next week.

I know you passed. I'm already planning your celebration.

Don't waste your breath filling up balloons.

If you'd stop stealing my breath away, I'd have more for balloons.

Cute line. Try again.

You're a hard audience.

I'm your favorite audience.

Truth. Love you.

Love you. Congrats again.

I pocket my phone and sit on the bench, watching practice. Just when I'm out of the limelight, I get pulled back in. But this time, it's not just about me. It's about the people and the town I love.

❦

THREE DAYS LATER, *SPORTSVERSE* ROLLS INTO TOWN. Word spread, and now I have a stadium full of bystanders. I've never had a closed practice, wanting to be as transparent as possible. Plus, there wasn't a need for it. Nobody, except a few dads, would linger around. But now I'm rethinking that decision.

"You're fine." Gillian pats my forehead with a tissue. "You've done interviews before. This is no different."

She's right, I've been on the other side of a camera plenty, but I thought I was done with it all. "Why don't we go under the bleachers and you can help me relax?"

She giggles and kisses my cheek. "Sorry, Noughton. Game face on."

Blythe Chen steps onto the track to the field.

"Back to the last name, huh?"

"Just when you're being uncooperative." Gillian's sweet smile pierces my heart. "Now I'm going to go sit with your dad and brothers and watch you kill this."

"Everyone does know that it's going to be, like, a five-minute segment, right?"

"Did you ever think that maybe people are here to support you?" She pokes me in the chest. Honestly, the thought hadn't come to mind. "They aren't here to get on camera, but to show the world how much they believe in you and this team."

I grab her, hating that I have to let her go. "How did I get so lucky to be with a woman so much smarter than me?"

She kisses my chin. Which I fucking love. "Easy. You won

her when she was a naïve teenager." She laughs again, kisses me one more time on the lips, and twirls out of my arms.

Blythe's eyes follow Gillian's retreat. "Girl back home story?"

I clear my throat. "Let's stick to football."

She smiles, still watching Gillian. I clear my throat again, and she brings her attention back to me. "All right. This is what's going to happen. Our guy is going to film the entire time. He'll get some B-roll footage to use for any voice-overs we might do. I'm going to go around and do the interviews. After we're done, I'll edit, and it will air. Easy peasy."

"Okay, sounds good."

"Do you mind if I walk around and grab a player here or there?"

"No. Go ahead." I motion to the field where they all are.

Blythe does exactly as she said. I'm interviewed for ten minutes, and she didn't ask one question about Gillian, which I'm thankful for.

Once they're done for the day, Blythe comes back over. "It will air next Thursday night. I'll send you an email. Thank you so much. It's very impressive what you've put together here."

"That one kid." The cameraman glances toward the junior varsity team. "Adams?"

My gut twists. "Yeah?"

"I can see that kid going pro someday. Got those hands." He shakes his head. "Unbelievable for his age."

Blythe leans to the left to get a better look at Clayton and jots his number on her pad. I'm close to saying don't spotlight the kid, but I keep my mouth shut.

"Yeah, he's got massive potential. Thank you, guys." I shake their hands, and they walk away.

They both wave to the stands, the cameraman filming as the Willowbrook residents chant, "Go Wildcats!"

ON THE THURSDAY THE SHOW AIRS, I SIT WITH
Gillian and Clayton in front of their television. We ordered
pizza, and it was as good an excuse as any to get Clayton to do
something with us. Although he's pretty much been on his
phone the entire time. He looks bored, but I have a feeling
he'll perk up if he sees himself on TV.

"It's going to be on soon." Gillian is giddier than anyone.

"Great." Clayton glances at the television and back at his
phone.

The segment comes on with a picture of me. "Next up,
where is Ben Noughton, San Francisco's star wide receiver,
now months after retirement?"

I lean back onto the couch, annoyed already. I'm not sure
why I feel that way, other than being retired makes me feel
fucking old.

Gillian is chewing on her piece of pizza five minutes later
when the piece comes on. She drops it onto her plate and hits
me in the thigh. "It's on."

"I'm not sleeping," I say with a chuckle.

"Jeez, Mom, calm down." Clayton turns his attention to
the television.

Blythe is in the studio when it starts. "Last week, we had
the opportunity to catch up with Ben Noughton." Clips of
some of my plays come on the screen, and most are some of
the best catches I made in my career. "The retired San Francisco wide receiver went back home to his small Nebraska
town known more for their cattle ranch farms than producing
professional football players." There's an aerial view of town.
"After his high school football coach suffered a heart attack,
Ben stepped into the role to make sure that this small team
didn't have to go without a season."

"Boy, they sure put a spin on it," Clayton says.

I agree with him. That's not quite how it all went down.

"He welcomed us to the field to watch his practice."

A clip of me blowing my whistle shows, then my face pops onto the screen from her interview with me. "I was once a Wildcat, and I'm happy to have the opportunity to coach a new group of Wildcats. It's about getting back to the roots, where the love of the game is bred while learning how to be a team player, relying on a group of guys all driven toward one single goal. It's fulfilling."

"I think part of the reason for Ben Noughton's smile might be the fact that he may have sparked a flame with his high school sweetheart." A picture of Gillian appears.

Clayton lets out an annoyed grunt.

"Oh god. I should have gotten a haircut like Coach Reyes," she says.

I put my arm around her and kiss her temple. "You look beautiful."

I notice Clayton watching us.

"And who are these boys Coach Noughton is spending so much of his time with? They're boys like number fourteen."

Clayton sits up in his chair.

Gillian looks at me as if I asked them to put him in.

They show multiple clips of Clayton running drills and catching the ball with ease. "I think we can all admit this kid is going places, and with a pro football wide receiver that will probably go to the Hall of Fame as his coach? Keep the name Clayton Adams in your head."

A clip starts with Coach Reyes and Coach Smith. Coach Reyes stares into the camera with his mouth hanging open.

"He brings new energy and a mentality of camaraderie and sportsmanship to the team. We're grateful to have him and know he'll lead us to the championships." Coach Smith elbows Coach Reyes.

He sways forward. "Yeah," Coach Reyes says.

"Oh, poor Coach Reyes." Gillian covers her mouth.

"I'm Blythe Chen, and thank you for watching *Sportsverse*. Next Thursday, join us while we talk to the head coach of the Chicago Grizzlies about his aspirations for his team next season."

Gillian mutes the television. "Whoa, Clay, the girls are going to be all over you now."

He shakes his head before he stares at me. "Did you pay them or something?"

"Clayton!"

"No," I say. "The cameraman came up to me at the end and complimented you. I thought they might mention you, but I didn't know for sure."

He nods, a small smile on his lips. His phone vibrates. "Drew." He holds it up and walks out of the room.

Gillian tackles me and pulls me to her, kissing my cheek. "You did great. I'd rather not have been a part of it, but both my boys did fantastic." She gives me a chaste kiss, then gets up and cleans up the pizza.

I follow her into the kitchen and lean against the counter as she puts away the leftovers.

"Any news?" I ask. The bar exam results are supposed to be announced any day now.

"Well." She cringes. "The results are in, but I didn't want to steal your moment, so..."

"Gillian!" I push off the counter, grabbing her laptop from the coffee table and bringing it to the kitchen table. "Log in."

"I don't know. I should open it alone. What if I failed?" Her hands shake, and I take them, running my hands over hers as if I'm warming them.

"Then you take it again. And it's me. I want to be here to support you either way."

She nods, and I lead her over to the table, sliding the chair out for her. She sits, opens her laptop, and sighs. She types in her password and waits before clicking on her email.

And there it is in her inbox.

My heart races, and I cross my fingers. She clicks, and I close my eyes.

"I passed," she says quietly. I open my eyes, and she turns toward me. "I passed!"

I shout and pick her up, swinging her around the room.

Clayton's door opens, and he comes in and stares at us. There isn't disgust in his face, but amazement, I think. "What's going on?"

"Your mom passed the bar exam!" I shout.

"Really?" He rushes over, and I release Gillian so he can hug her.

She clings to him.

"Congratulations, Mom," he says.

"Thank you." She steps back and wipes away her tears.

"I guess I'll be using all my breath to blow up balloons now." I grin.

Gillian laughs, and Clayton looks at me as though I'm the stupidest person to ever walk the planet.

I'm so happy, you'd think I just passed the bar. Actually, you'd think I was just inducted into the Hall of Fame.

Chapter Twenty-Six

BEN

I walk into The Knotted Barn to check things out before the festivities begin. Romy's done an amazing job decorating for the party I'm throwing for Gillian.

"I hope when Laurel brings her here, she's not thinking this is some surprise proposal."

Romy glances over her shoulder, spreading congratulations confetti on the high tables around the dance floor. "Laurel is telling her that it's girls' night out. She probably has some plan to sneak out and find you."

"You're funny. We haven't been that attached."

Romy stops, dramatically dropping the confetti around the vases of flowers. "You have, but everyone understands. Well... everyone but Clayton, I've heard. Not that you can blame him."

"Yeah, yeah, I left her..."

She stares at me with raised eyebrows. "I was going to say, it's his mom. Aren't all boys protective of their moms?"

I shrug, frowning. "Not sure I would know."

She nods and gives me an apologetic look because she still has both of her parents. "He'll come around."

"That's what everyone says."

She walks by, running her hand down my arm. "I know patience isn't always your thing, but in this case, you have to be."

I clap my hands, done with the conversation.

"Whoa." Brooks walks in. "Romy, this is great." He's dressed in jeans, cowboy boots, a plaid shirt, and a cowboy hat. "Pulling out all the stops, huh?"

I shake my head at Brooks. "It's a big day. She was always a supporter of my dreams. I want to show her that it's her turn and I'm happy to stand by her side while she crushes them."

His eyes crinkle. "Are you reading romance books?"

My forehead furrows. "Why?"

"Those sound like lines from one."

"How would you know?" I ask, tilting my head.

His cheeks turn red. "Hey, it's boring sometimes at the station. And Aimee, the dispatcher, reads them. Occasionally, she leaves one behind. It's not like—"

I put up my hand. "You can stop now."

He blows out a breath. "When's everyone else getting here?"

"You mean, when is Lottie getting here?" I pat his shoulder. "What's up with you two?"

"Since I don't know if she's going to be here, nothing."

"But you want something to happen?"

His eyes veer left.

"Left!" I shout, pointing at him.

Brooks used to tell everyone that someone is lying if they look left when asked a question.

He shakes his head as if I'm not right.

"She's going to love it!" a woman's voice says, and Brooks is saved by Betsy, her family, and Clayton. Betsy walks over and hugs me. "You did a great job."

Romy raises her hand. "He didn't do anything but cut a check."

"And invites. And if Gillian asks, I blew up the balloons."

"You have helium in those lungs?" Betsy asks.

"I don't want to know your kinky shit." Romy climbs down from the ladder. "Sorry, Clayton."

He eyes me for a second, then Drew nudges Clayton, and they go out to the balcony that looks out over the small vineyard.

"He'll get there." Betsy pats me on the shoulder.

Next, my dad and Emmett, along with Lottie, walk in. I glance at Brooks.

"Fuck off," Brooks says under his breath.

Soon the room fills with more people, and I grow more anxious for Gillian to get here.

My cousin Jenson cooks amazing food, and his appetizers are going as if these people haven't eaten in a month. He brings in another tray from The Getaway Lodge where his big kitchen is.

"Thanks, Jenson," I say, stealing a cheese puff. I'm starving myself.

"It was crazy, right? I mean, Waylon Knight." Brooks is off to the side, talking to Jude. When I look over, Brooks is shaking his head.

My body goes rigid. Jenson places the tray on the appetizer table, and I eavesdrop on Brooks's conversation with Jude.

"Last I heard, he spent all the money his grandma left him. After she died, he dug little holes all over her yard to see if she'd buried more." Jude shakes his head and tips his beer to his lips.

"He didn't even recognize me. I get that I was in my sheriff's uniform, but—"

"What did you say?" I ask. "About Waylon?"

"Shit, remember the crap you two gave each other?" Brooks slaps me on the back.

"He was such an asshole," Jude says. "I hate the idea he's only a few towns away."

"Only a few towns?" I ask, needing clarity on exactly how close he is.

"Yeah, I was down at the county courthouse," Brooks says. "Guess he got a ticket for driving without a license. The guy was always fucking up."

"So, he's in jail then?"

Brooks and Jude both scrunch their eyebrows at me, maybe hearing something in my tone.

"Why? You want a reunion with him?" Brooks asks.

"Fuck no. I was just wondering." I shrug, trying to play it off.

Brooks relaxes, but Jude's appraising eye says he knows I'm hung up about something.

"I don't know. He was walking out, so he must've gotten off." Brooks's eyes light up. "He did ask about you, though. Saw that segment on TV. Probably rubbed him the wrong way. He was always so jealous of you."

"He asked about me?" The hair on the back of my neck stands up.

"About you being back. Asked if you and Gillian are back together."

I lift my cowboy hat and run my hand through my hair. This isn't good. "What did you tell him?"

"I said you're back and you and Gillian are as hot and heavy as ever."

A nauseous feeling runs through my stomach, and bile rises up my throat.

"You okay, Ben?" Jude asks.

I open my mouth to say I'm good.

"Laurel just texted. They've parked and are on their way

up the hill in the UTV," Lottie shouts loudly enough so the whole room can hear her.

I leave Brooks and Jude and head to the open area to wait. I force myself to put the Waylon thing out of my mind so I can put all my attention on Gillian tonight.

Everyone stares at the door. It's not her birthday, so we're not going to turn off the lights and say surprise. Hopefully she doesn't kill me for planning this big party. Gillian isn't a flashy or braggy person, but this is a celebration of her accomplishments, which took a lot of fucking work on her part. I'm so proud of her.

"Clay." I wave him over to join me.

"Clayton," he clarifies.

I'm not sure if and when this kid will come around.

The doors open, and Laurel and Gillian step in.

"Congratulations!" everyone screams.

Gillian covers her mouth. She's wearing another sundress, a simple one that goes down to her ankles, and I half wonder if she knew where she was going tonight. I walk toward her, and she wraps her arms around me.

"You knew?" I whisper.

"No."

I draw back, and the truth is all over her face. She knew.

"How are those lungs?" she asks, rising to kiss me.

"Turns out Romy's got a helium tank."

She laughs and sees Clayton behind me. "Clay!"

She leaves me and goes to him.

"I didn't do anything. He did it all." Clayton thumbs in my direction.

Gillian exhales a deep breath and looks over her shoulder at me. I guess I should've asked him to help, but I didn't think about it. Maybe it's not only Clayton who's holding us back from coming together.

GILLIAN FLITS AROUND THE ROOM, A SMILE ON HER face as people praise her for the hard work and dedication she had to becoming a lawyer. She gets drilled with a lot of questions regarding where she'll go and if she's leaving Willowbrook. People keep telling her our town needs our own lawyer because everyone is done with the one in Hickory. Sometimes her eyes find me across the room, and she shrugs and says one step at a time.

Clayton and Drew walk over to the dessert table. Laurel did a fantastic job with the cake. It's a three-tier black cake with the scales of justice in gold icing drawn on the side. She topped it with a diploma and graduation cap.

I walk over and join the boys. "Can I talk to you for a second, Clayton?"

He looks at Drew. Drew nods like "give him a chance." Thanks, Drew.

"Sure," Clayton says.

I walk us out to the balcony. Gillian clocks it. I'm sure she wants to join us, but she doesn't move from where she is. Her trust in me still surprises me.

I look over the vineyard that my uncle started. It's not large, and we only produce a small amount of wine every year, but it's cool to have a winery in Nebraska.

"I want to apologize. I should've involved you in the planning."

He shrugs. "It's fine."

"No, it's not. Listen, I care for your mom, and she... I would like us to form some kind of relationship."

"You're my coach. That's a relationship."

"You know what I mean."

"Fine." He's doing it for his mom and not going willingly.

"You know, I'd love to work with you on some drills."

"Okay. Can I go now?" He crosses his arms.

"Yeah." I blow out a breath.

Brooks follows Clayton with his eyes as he walks out onto the balcony and Clayton walks back inside. "That kid needs a swift kick in the ass. Could you imagine what our dads would do?"

I rest my arms on the balcony. "I fucked it up. Maybe he'll always hate me."

Brooks slaps me on the back. "You're too good of a guy for him to hate you *all* of his life."

Good guy. I don't feel like it right now. And then I'm reminded about Waylon.

"Hey." I glance behind me, not seeing anyone. "I need you to do something for me."

"I'm not babysitting the kid so you can fuck Gillian again."

I laugh. "Hey, I'll repay you at some point. And I got you donuts and coffee."

His nostrils flare, and he nods at me, shoving his hands in his pockets. "What do you want?"

"Waylon Knight."

He looks right and left. "What about him?"

I lean in closer. "I need to know where he's living. Is he really two towns away?"

"Why?" Brooks frowns.

"I can't tell you."

His shoulders fall. "Listen, this isn't babysitting a kid. This is using police resources to find information on someone without a good reason. It's kind of unethical, man."

I hate putting my friend in a bad position. It's not like me to ever ask, but I'm desperate. If Waylon returns here to start trouble and I'm the one who drew him here because of that stupid segment, I'll never forgive myself. I need to make sure he stays the hell out of Willowbrook and out of Gillian and

Clayton's lives. The guy is bad news, and Gillian has made it clear she wants nothing to do with him.

Brooks has always been a great friend to me. He's kept secrets for me before. I weigh the idea of telling him against the idea of Waylon showing up unannounced and decide the latter is worse.

"If I tell you, you can't tell anyone."

"You know you can trust me." He moves closer.

I take a few steps away from the door, double-checking that no one is there. "Clayton's dad—"

"It's you! I always knew it."

I shake my head. "No. It's not me. It's..." I lean in and lower my voice. "Waylon Knight."

"Fuck off." He hits me in the chest, shock etched in his features. "Gillian and Waylon?"

I nod. "But... the thing is, and I swear to God, Brooks, I'm only telling you this because if he steps foot in this town to cause her or Clayton shit, you'll be arresting me for murder."

His head rears back. "He's an alcoholic and petty thief. Why would you murder him?"

I blow out a breath and look out to the vineyard. What kind of a man would I be if I didn't protect the woman I love and her son?

"He hit Gillian."

"Fuck off." He hits me in the chest again.

"Can you please stop doing that?" I rub my chest.

He shakes his head, mulling it over. "I'll look him up tonight after the party. If he does come back here, I'm your backup. I always knew he was an asshole, but to hit a woman?"

"Clayton!"

Brooks and I both look up. Drew is walking over to where Clayton is standing in the balcony doorway, his face pale and his mouth open.

"Clayton," I say, pushing Brooks out of the way.

But Clayton turns around and storms back into the party.

"Clayton!" I call again, gaining the attention of everyone, including Gillian.

She watches her son as he barrels toward her, her face growing more concerned with each step. "What happened?" she mouths to me.

"Is it true?" Clayton says.

"Is what true?" She shakes her head, having no idea what's going on.

"That my dad is some deadbeat named Waylon Knight and that he hit you?"

Gasps fill the room. I close my eyes, not wanting to open them for fear of what I'm going to see on Gillian's face.

Chapter Twenty-Seven

GILLIAN

I'm talking with Betsy and some of the other moms I've been friends with since the boys were in preschool, chatting about memories of when the boys were younger and how old they've gotten. Betsy brings up Kait and Clayton because Drew says they're talking a lot. I guess I'm not as involved in my kid's life as I think. Or he's just hiding it from me.

I hear Ben call Clayton's name, and the crowd turns toward the doors that open to the balcony. Clayton's storming toward me, Ben following. Did Ben push too hard with Clay? Was my son rude or disrespectful? I thought things were heading in the right direction. Clay actually asked me about Ben the other day.

Now Clayton is standing in front of me looking as if he's about one second from crying. His eyes are welling up, and his nose is crinkling.

"Is it true?" Clayton says.

"Is what true?" I shake my head. What the heck has him so upset?

"That my dad is some deadbeat named Waylon Knight and that he hit you?"

Gasps fill the room, and my stomach sinks to the floor.

"Did he?"

Everyone's attention is on us, and I'm so stunned I'm not sure how to react. "I—"

"Mom?"

"Come here." I put my arm around him and escort him outside the barn.

Ben steps forward, but I put out my hand. He's done enough damage from what I suspect.

Bruce walks past us and stands by Ben. He can take care of his son while I take care of mine.

Once I get Clayton outside, I walk us farther away from the barn so no one sees or hears what we're saying. "Okay, Clay."

"Is it true?" He releases the tears he's been holding back, and they cascade down his cheeks. "That my dad was an asshole, an alcoholic?"

"It's complicated," I say, unprepared to be discussing this. Especially right now.

"It's not, Mom! You said you'd always be honest, and you kept all this from me!" His voice grows louder.

I push away my own tears because one of us has to be strong right now.

"You can't yell at your mom," Ben says, walking over.

Clayton's eyes veer away. He's obviously embarrassed to be seen crying.

I sigh and look at Ben. "Not now, Ben. Please. Just give us some space."

"I'm sorry. I'm sorry that he overheard me. I didn't mean to—"

"But you did," I say, my voice shuddering. "I need to handle Clayton right now."

Ben backs off, but he lingers in the distance.

"I'm sorry, Clay. I thought I was saving you from heartbreak. You didn't need to know that. It makes no difference because he's never returned, and he probably won't."

"Then why is Ben asking Brooks to look him up? He mentioned murder."

My shoulders fall, and I glare at Ben. "Let's just go home, okay?"

Clayton nods, clearly eager to get away from here.

It's then that I realize I have no car here. Clayton walks toward the parking lot while I stop in front of Ben. "Can you please get Laurel for me?"

"I'll take you home. Let me fix this."

"Please, Ben, I can't right now." He needs to stop pushing me or I'm going to go mama bear on him.

"Gillian. I didn't mean—"

"What, Ben?" I shout. "You didn't mean to tell everyone in there my biggest secret? My son? Jesus, what were you thinking?"

"I was thinking that I wanted to keep you both safe. That my stupid segment was drawing him back here and it was going to blow up in your face. I was trying to stop that from happening."

My arms flail out at my sides. "Congratulations, you're the one who blew it up."

"Don't. Gillian."

"What? Don't what?"

"I made a mistake. I should have talked to you first. I'm sorry."

"You think? But Ben does what he always does. Whatever he wants."

He takes off his cowboy hat and runs his hand through his hair. "You're going to throw my past mistakes in my face?"

Laurel comes out, probably hearing the screaming, and she sees Clayton heading to the parking lot. I nod, and she walks toward him.

"I have to go take care of my son. Maybe we can talk later."
I walk away.

Ben takes my hand, his thumb running along my inner
wrist. "Gill."

"I can't."

He releases his grip, and my hand falls to my side.

I walk to the car, finally allowing the tears to fall.

I LET CLAYTON HAVE ONE NIGHT TO SLEEP ON THE
news before we address everything.

Ben texted and called all night long, but I didn't answer
him. I can't right now. I'm embarrassed that the entire town
knows I slept with Waylon Knight. That he hit me. Mostly,
I'm embarrassed that my son knows, and Ben's the reason
for it.

I knock on Clayton's door, and he mumbles, "Come in."

He's on his bed, his phone in his hands.

"I made French toast with strawberries. Want some?"

"I'm not really hungry."

"Clay, please."

He blows out a breath, not looking at me. "Give me a
minute."

I shut the door and go back into the kitchen, where I set
the two plates on the kitchen table. Clayton comes in wearing
shorts and a Willowbrook Wildcats tank top. He sits in his
usual chair, and I sit in mine.

"I want to apologize. You're right that I lied, and I
shouldn't have. I have a million buts I want to say, but I'm not
going to because if I expect you to be truthful with me, then I
have to be truthful with you even if it's going to hurt you."

He picks up his fork. "Thanks."

"I thought I was saving you from being hurt. It was bad

enough he left, that he didn't care that I was pregnant, but after he… hit me." I suck back my tears as Clayton puts down his fork. "I knew I didn't want him in either of our lives, and it was best to let him leave. And we've been good, right?"

He nods.

"Do you have any questions?"

"Are you going to answer anything I ask?"

I nod, drawing a deep breath to stifle my nerves. "Yeah. If you want to know something, I'll tell you."

"Who already knew about my dad?"

"Laurel and Ben."

"That's it?" He arches an eyebrow.

"That's it. Now the entire town knows." Anger flows through my veins.

"Can you tell me anything about him?"

"Sure, what little I know. Waylon Knight was a year older than me. When he graduated, he left Willowbrook, but his grandma died. He was raised by her, and I'm not sure I know why, unfortunately. But when she died, he had to come back and settle her estate since he was the beneficiary. That's when I saw him at the bar. I was about a month off the breakup with Ben—"

"Can we fast-forward to you finding out you're pregnant?"

I sniffle. "Yeah. Of course." I take a moment and sip my coffee. "Waylon and I snuck around a couple times, and he had a quick temper. He would disappear and come back to town. Never wanted to answer my questions. I was ready to tell him I was done when I found out I was about five weeks pregnant. He thought it was Ben's, and he hit me. Said that I was trying to trap him."

Clayton's chest heaves up and down. *Hold on, kid, we're almost done.*

"Then he apologized and said he didn't mean it. That he

was drunk. So I gave him one more chance. Another night, he drank too much and hit me again."

I'm not going into specifics. He doesn't need the visual in his head.

"And that's when I told him we were done. He left town and never came back. I suspect because he doesn't want to... well, I can't say why, but that's it."

"Sheriff Watson said he was always jealous of Ben?"

I nod. "He was."

"Do you ever wonder if that's why he hit on you that night at the bar?"

I shrug. "I'm not sure."

He eats half his French toast, not speaking, and I allow him to soak in all the information.

"Mom?"

"Yeah?"

"They say that it can be passed down. I mean, do you think that I'll be like him?"

"Oh, Clayton." I rush over and slide out of the chair next to his, taking his head in my hands and laying it on my shoulder. "You should be concerned about the alcoholism. Addiction can run in families. But the hitting does not. It's a learned behavior. You have the choice to do it or not. And I know you. You're not like that. It's one reason I never wanted him back in our lives."

"Okay." He pulls back from me, wiping tears from his eyes. "You're okay now?"

I nod. "Perfect."

"What are you going to do about Ben?"

I pat his shoulder. "Don't worry about that."

"He made you happy, though."

I stand and tuck the chair under the table. "He did. Yes."

"You're using past tense."

"I promised to be honest, so all I can tell you is that I don't have the answers right now. I have a lot of thinking to do." I sit in my chair and force myself to eat a bite of my French toast.

"He said he was trying to protect you... us?"

I look at him skeptically. "Are you Team Ben now?"

He shakes his head. "I'm just saying what I heard."

I put my napkin on the table. "I don't expect you to understand this, but I trusted Ben, and I wish he would've come to me. He chose to handle it on his own, and that's not fair when you're in a relationship and it's going to affect the other person. You communicate with one another." I pick up my dish and walk over to the sink.

Two arms wrap around my shoulders. "Thanks for being a great mom. I love you."

I pat his hands. "I love you too." I turn around and rest my hands on the counter behind me. "So, now it's your turn to confess all. What's going on with Kait?"

He laughs, and I've never wanted to hear that sound more than I do right now.

Chapter Twenty-Eight

BEN

A WEEK LATER...

I walk into the kitchen and find my dad sitting at the table, which is strange since it's not Sunday.

"Gillian still not answering you?" he asks.

I shake my head and pour myself a coffee. "I was just trying to—"

"Yeah, love makes people do stupid things, but your thing was selfish *and* stupid."

"Gee, thanks, Dad. I gotta go shower."

"Sit down, Ben."

We don't ever turn our backs on our dad, so I pull out the old kitchen chair my dad hasn't replaced since I was a kid.

"I know why you did it, and I should have had this conversation with you earlier. Your mom is probably shouting at me right now. You've been by yourself and made your own decisions all these years. You didn't have to think of anyone but yourself. And you love Gillian, and you want to be a family with Gillian and Clayton, no?"

I nod.

"You thought you were helping. Taking it off her plate. But women... they don't want that. If it's going to affect the family, you communicate with her and come to the decision together."

"Didn't you, like, knock some guy on his ass when he hit on Mom once?" I arch an eyebrow.

"That's not what I'm talking about. That's jealousy, and your mom pretended to be mad, but she didn't want that creep anywhere near her. I wasn't going to look at your mom and say, 'Should I hit him?'"

I shake my head. "You're confusing me."

"What you did didn't affect you two for one night. It was deep. You shared a secret that she's been keeping for years. And I assume you weren't going to tell her that you knew Waylon was two towns over?"

I shrug.

"It's the secrets, Ben. Secrets don't have any place in a relationship. Now that you've tried to keep it a secret and it all came out, Gillian's trust in you has been severed."

"That's a little severe."

"Severed means severe, Ben."

I throw my hands in the air. "I know, Dad." I sound like an asshole teenager, and my dad shoots me his warning glare.

"You have to give her time to come to terms with what happened. If she loves you, she will."

"You expect me to just sit around here? I've waited a fucking week. Hell, I've waited fifteen years."

"If you don't want to wait, then you have to go after her. But words aren't going to do it. Only actions."

"Like what?" I ask.

He stands, sipping his coffee. Then he dumps the remainder in the sink and rinses the cup. "If I told you, it wouldn't mean anything. You're a smart boy. You went to Clemson. Figure it out." He walks out the back door, but it springs open again a second later.

"I got it, Dad."

"Out of the way." Emmett runs through the kitchen and up the stairs.

It's a good reminder to finish my fucking house.

❦

It's our first football game and everyone in Willowbrook is out and in the stands.

It's killing me that Gillian is up there and still not talking to me.

Junior varsity plays first. And of course, Clayton is the star player.

I see a person standing along the fence line, but they're in the shadows. I can't see their face.

"Who's that?" I ask Coach Smith since Coach Reyes is busy coaching junior varsity to their victory.

He follows where I'm looking and shrugs. "Not sure. I've never known someone to stand away from everyone." Coach Smith looks behind us. "There's still some room on the bleachers."

The hairs on the back of my neck raise, and for the first time tonight, I look up at Gillian. I don't know how I've managed to resist this long. She's clueless, standing and cheering with everyone else because Clayton just caught a touchdown in the end zone.

My dad's words come back to me. This doesn't just affect me. This affects Gillian and Clayton, so for the rest of the game, I watch the shadow, hoping like hell I'm wrong.

Junior varsity wins their game, and since they have to stay

for the varsity game, they take the bench as the varsity players get ready.

I'm busy coaching the varsity boys, but I track the person growing closer to the fence opening the further the game progresses. Varsity wins, and everyone in Willowbrook cheers and yells, chanting "Wildcats!" over and over.

On our way off the field, I fall into line with Clayton. "Great job tonight."

He makes eye contact with me, and they're the same eyes as his mom's. My heart pinches at the thought that she may never talk to me again. "Thanks, Coach Noughton."

All the fans clap as the players go by. As they exit through the fence to head back into the school and take showers and change, the shadow emerges, and my worst fear comes true.

Waylon Knight stands there, clapping like every other fan, except his eyes are only on one person. "Fourteen."

Clayton doesn't hear him. He's talking to his mentors, who are patting him on the back.

"Hey, fourteen!"

Clayton stops, looks to his right, and slows, letting the pack go ahead of him. I stay back and put my hand on Coach Smith to stay with me. I glance at Gillian, who sees what's about to happen. She's pushing through the crowd, not letting her eyes stray from her son.

"Heck of a job out there," Waylon says.

I'm not sure if Clayton sees it, but they have a similar nose and jawline. Not everyone would suspect that they're father and son, but now, side by side, it's hard not to see it.

"Clay!" Gillian shouts, sprinting down the side of the field.

Clayton turns to his mom. He must notice her panic and can probably read his mom better than I can. I figure he'll look back at Waylon and connect the dots, but his eyes search me out instead. In them, there's one question.

I nod.

"Who are you?" Clayton asks.

"Is that who I think it is?" Coach Smith asks from next to me.

"Yeah." I step forward a few more paces to break the distance since Gillian hasn't been able to get here yet.

Coach Smith comes shoulder to shoulder with me.

Waylon says, "You don't know me, but... jeez, I can't believe how amazing you were out there. Impressive."

My dad steps next to me as my brothers saunter over and stand shoulder to shoulder with Coach Smith. All of us have our arms crossed, staring Waylon down.

"Who are you?" Clayton asks again, not thanking Waylon for his compliment like he normally would.

Waylon looks past Clayton at Gillian, approaching slowly now that she's close enough. He probably wants to see how this is going to play out before answering. "I'm your dad."

"You're Waylon Knight?" Clayton asks.

"And here I thought I was your mom's dirty little secret."

I turn my hat backward and step forward, but my dad puts his hand on my stomach to stop me.

He has to be kidding me.

"So, you're him." Clayton looks at me again.

I'm not sure why he keeps seeking me out.

Gillian comes up next to her son. "What are you doing here?"

"I saw your boyfriend's little segment on TV. Looks like you and me did good. He's a star player."

"She—" I start to say, but my dad shakes his head again. Fucking hell.

Gillian glances at me—the first time her eyes have been on me in over a week. But I can't read her. I don't know what she wants me to do.

"You didn't do anything but donate sperm," Gillian says.

"Come on, son, I'm back. I thought you'd want to see me. What nasty stories has your mom told you about me?"

I finally step out of the circle, and my dad willingly lets me go this time. "That's enough, Waylon. Get the hell outta here."

He turns to me, and his hair is greasy and long. His teeth are yellow and stained, one is missing. And he stinks of alcohol.

"This doesn't have anything to do with you, Noughton. Nice welcome sign, by the way." He laughs, and there's more than one tooth missing.

I hate that Clayton has to see his dad in this condition.

"It does." My jaw tics.

His head falls back. "Oh, that's right. You two are back together. How cute. A story for the ages. But see, this boy is mine. Not yours. I bet that fucking burns you up inside, doesn't it?" He grins and puts his hand on Clayton's shoulder, and I break the distance.

Clayton shrugs off the hand. "I have a question."

"What is it, son?"

By now, everyone is circled around, making it appear as though it's the town of Willowbrook against Waylon Knight. As it should be.

"Did you hit my mom?"

Grunts echo in the night air under the lights. Gillian glances around.

Waylon glares at Gillian. "Did she tell you that? She's a lying bitch."

I cock my fist back, but before I can land a punch, Clayton's fist connects with Waylon's face. Gillian's eyes bulge, and her mouth falls open.

Holy shit.

"Fuck, son, you can even hit." Waylon puts his hand on

his chin and wiggles it back and forth. "But it doesn't change that you're mine."

A sheriff's car pulls into the parking lot with the lights on but no sirens. Brooks steps out in full uniform. "Okay. Enough everyone." He takes out his cuffs. "Waylon Knight, you can't be intoxicated on school property. I'm taking you into the station."

"What? Fucking Barney Fife, get your hands off me."

Brooks puts the cuffs on Waylon. "Don't make me add resisting arrest."

"This is some small-town bullshit. It doesn't matter, Gillian, he's mine, and I'll be back."

Gillian inhales deeply and takes Clayton's hand. Clayton shakes his other hand.

"Let's get you an ice pack," I say.

Surprisingly, he kisses his mom on the cheek. "I'll be right back."

"Okay."

Laurel comes up to Gillian, putting her arm around her shoulders. Lottie and Romy join them. At least she has a group of people to support her if she won't let me be there.

On the way into the locker room, I don't say much because I'm sure this is hard on Clayton, and he's not a fan of mine.

"Sorry," he mumbles.

"Nothing to be sorry for. You're not in trouble. Don't worry." I open the door to the locker room.

"I meant you wanted to hit him, right?"

I chuckle. "Yeah, but..."

"You wanted to impress Mom?"

I shake my head. "No. I wanted to hurt the fucker who hurt your mom."

He stops for a second, holding the hand that threw the punch.

I get him an ice pack, and the team surrounds him, asking questions about what happened.

I head into my office and shut the door to calm myself because I really want to beat that shithead to a pulp. And I have no idea what's going on in Gillian's head now.

Chapter Twenty-Nine

BEN

I knock on Gillian's door. Her car is in the driveway, so I know she's home. My hands shake, so I put them in my pockets.

She opens the door and doesn't say anything, but she opened the door. That has to be a good sign.

"Can we talk?"

She nods and steps to the side.

"Is Clayton home?" I ask.

"No, he's Mister Hot Shot since he punched his dad. Out with Kait."

I give her a small smile and step into the house. "It was an impressive punch."

"His hand is swollen, but he tells me he's fine." She motions to the couch. "Do you want a drink?"

"No, thanks."

I sit on the couch, and she sits on the chair. Just that feels crushing. I miss her cuddling up into me on the couch.

"First of all, I'm sorry, Gillian. I acted selfishly when I went behind your back and told Brooks to look into Waylon. I should've come to you with my worries so we could handle them together."

She sighs. "Ben, we're a team. If we're together, I have to be able to trust that you're not hiding stuff from me. Even if you're trying to protect me."

"I know. My dad—"

"Good ol' Bruce."

"I'm giving you time to forgive me. I won't pressure you, but you should know that I'm so damn sorry. I'd do about anything to take it back."

She stares at me, and I can't read her. It's frustrating as hell. "I know you would, and thank you. In the end, it's probably for the best. It's kind of a weight off my shoulders. Clayton knows now, and..." She rolls her eyes. "The whole town too."

I wince and nod. "I'm here for a different reason, though."

She rears her head back. "Oh, what?"

"Waylon isn't going to go away. He thinks Clayton is his ticket to money and fame. Brooks overhead him telling another guy in jail how his kid is going places and a bunch of other shit that could just be him running his mouth, but it might not be."

"He'll never win custody." Her voice is strong, but I see the worry in her eyes.

"True. But he could make Clayton's and your life hell."

She nibbles the inside of her cheek. "So? What do you think we should do?"

"I want to pay him off."

She bolts off the chair. "Ben."

"I know what you're going to say, but with people like Waylon, money works. I pay him, and he signs away any rights to Clayton. It's a win."

She paces the room. "I can't ask you to do that. I don't

even know where we stand. I just interviewed in Lincoln this week. We might move. And—"

"I told you I'd go with you. If you want me to." I clear my throat.

Gillian shakes her head. "I'm not taking you away from your family again."

"You're not taking me away. I'm choosing to go with you." I stand and break the distance between us. "I don't care if you never talk to me again. I mean, I care. I really fucking care. You'll break my heart in two. It'll be irreparable. I'll never come back from it."

I get a small smile from her.

"The money is worth it if I know that you and Clayton are safe." I hold my breath, hoping she'll agree.

"I would have to pay you back."

I huff. "No, you wouldn't."

"Ben..."

"Hey, you're mad that I didn't go to you first before I talked to Brooks. This isn't your problem, Gillian, it's *our* problem. If you want us to be together, then this is me telling you, I heard you, and I'm changing."

She rubs her forehead. "Do you really think the money would help?"

I nod. "Yes."

"How much are you going to offer him?"

"As much as it takes. I'm sure ten grand will do. Guys like him are shortsighted." I'd pay him ten times that to go away forever, but I don't say that. We can discuss it if it comes to that.

"Ten grand? Ben?" She shakes her head. "I can't let you do that."

"Listen, one day when you forgive me and you agree to marry me, my money will be your money. So you can consider it an investment in our future." I grin at her.

"That cocky smirk. Who said I was going to forgive you, let alone marry you?"

I shrug. "Call it a gut feeling."

She inhales and stares at me. "I have to talk to Clayton."

"Okay. You talk to him and let me know." I turn to go to the door. "I'll be waiting for you, Gillian, always." I grab the doorknob.

"Noughton."

I shake my head and turn back around.

"We do things together. We'll talk to Clayton together."

My lips turn up. I want to run to her, but she's still closed off, so I stay put.

"He's going to be home in a couple of minutes. Do you want to wait?" she asks.

"I'd love to." I sit on the couch, unsure where we fit right now.

Thankfully, Clayton comes home shortly, stopping in the doorway and staring at us. "What now?"

"We need to talk," Gillian says.

"Is Ben my new daddy?" He says it in a voice that makes me want to laugh.

"Cute. Sit." Gillian points at the spot next to me.

He sits and tosses his phone on the coffee table.

"Ben has a solution for Waylon. He came here to ask my permission before he did it, and I told him we make decisions together now and there aren't secrets, right?"

Clayton nods.

"Go ahead, Ben." Gillian puts out her hand for me to talk.

"Me?" I ask, thumbing my chest.

"Yes." Gillian sits back in the chair, crossing her arms.

"I was telling your mom that Sheriff Watson heard your... Waylon talking about how he thinks you're the next big thing and that you're going to make him rich. How talented you are and that you're his son."

A look of disgust forms on Clayton's face.

I take a deep breath. "I want to offer him money to sign papers that says he's giving up any rights to you. Obviously, I'd like him to stay away for good, and I hope he doesn't bother you after you turn eighteen. But this gets him out of you and your mom—"

"Our," Gillian says.

"What?" I look at her.

"It's not just Clayton and me. It's your life too. Our life."

I smile, but Clayton's forehead is scrunched up as if his mom and I are talking in code.

"But it gets him out of our life," I finish.

Clayton shrugs. "Cool."

"That's it?" Gillian asks, mouth gaping.

Clayton stands and grabs his phone. "I don't want any part of him, and whatever gets him away from"—he looks between me and his mom—"*us* is good with me."

Gillian nods. "All right then."

"I'm heading to my room." He walks toward the hallway but stops and turns around. "Thanks, Ben."

Gillian's eyes widen.

I give him a nod. "You're welcome."

Clayton leaves, and I release my first full breath since Gillian and I stopped talking.

Then I stand. "I'm going to go now. Brooks said he's in some hotel on the outskirts of town."

"I should go with you." She stands and goes to get her purse.

"Sorry, but no, you shouldn't. I understand that we make decisions together, but I'm asking you, Gillian, to allow me to do this. I have Jude and Emmett ready to go with me. I don't want you anywhere near him."

She holds her purse to her body. "Okay. Thanks, Ben."

I relax a little that she has the confidence to trust me to

handle this. "You don't have to thank me. This is for us, right?" My question is to see where we stand.

"Yes. Let's find a time to talk."

"I'll call you."

She nods.

I walk out the door feeling as though we have to put Waylon behind us before we can move forward. At least she's opened the door for me to step back in.

Chapter Thirty

GILLIAN

I go out to start my car, but it won't turn over.

"What the heck?"

I pop the hood, but who am I kidding? I know nothing about cars.

"Hey, Gilly Be!" Emmett pulls up along the curb.

I look around. "Why are you on my street?"

"I just came from someone's house." He puts his finger to his lips. "Our secret." He winks and laughs in his usual contagious chuckle. "When are you going to forgive my brother?"

I shake my head. "We're meeting for dinner tonight."

"Ah. Then you're going to go at it like rabbits. He's really been hitting it in the shower lately."

It will take a special lady to deal with Emmett and how he doesn't think before he opens his mouth.

"Could you look at my car?" I ask. "It won't start."

"Sure." He parks and hops out. Emmett is the tallest Noughton, but he still has that boyish grin. He looks under my hood. "I'm gonna be honest, Gilly Be, I don't know much about cars."

I chuckle. "Don't you work on the tractors?"

"Tractors aren't cars," he says as if I'm five.

"I'm aware, but I thought engines and stuff were pretty much the same."

"Sorry, but I'll take you wherever you want to go." He heads down the driveway toward his truck.

"Um... I was going to shop."

"Perfect. I love shopping. Come on. We should bond because we both know you're going to be my sister-in-law."

"I am?"

"One day."

I shrug. He has a point, although I already feel pretty close to him. I grab my purse, shut my hood, and lock up my car.

"Emmett, have you ever heard of a garbage can?" I ask as I get in his truck.

He picks up a fast-food bag from the passenger seat and tosses it in the back. "Yeah, it's my back seat."

I sit and wait for him to start driving.

"Gilly Be, we don't drive without seat belts."

"Oh yeah." I reach for the seat belt and slide a box of condoms to the side. "Please tell me you don't have sex in here?"

He laughs and presses the gas. My back jolts to the back of the seat. "No. I picked those up last night. The girl seemed feisty, but turns out she was a one-and-done."

"I love you, Emmett, but I hope you never date my sister or my friend."

He doesn't say anything, but he turns the opposite way of the shopping area.

"Emmett, you're going the wrong way."

"I didn't know we were going shopping. I gotta get my wallet."

I sigh. "Are you driving without your license?"

He doesn't answer right away. "Don't tell Sheriff Watson. Or do." He shrugs.

Emmett's never been a rule-follower. It's just not in his nature. But pushing the boundaries? That's in his nature.

He pulls down the long road that leads to Plain Daisy Ranch, and I place my hand over my stomach.

"Relax, it's fine. Benny's not home," he says.

We pass the family house, and he turns into the drive that circles the lake. I'm not sure I remember the way back here, but I'm pretty sure when he takes the first left, something is up.

"Emmett?"

"It's a shortcut." He nods, both of our asses bumping up and down on the ripped vinyl seats.

Then he stops the truck in front of a path of rose petals.

"What is this?" I ask.

"This is where our ride stops. Follow the rose petals to the yellow brick road."

I open the door and he chuckles, always finding his own jokes hilarious.

"Am I going to be murdered?"

"No. But you might be taken. Be on the lookout for a big guy with a lot of muscle. Kind of a dopey lovesick look on his face. He's gonna snatch you up and never let you go, like King Kong and that little woman."

I sigh. "Thanks for the ride, Emmett."

He winks, and I shut the door. I follow the path, and music starts to play as I grow closer to where I know Ben is building his house. "Change Your Name" by Brett Young plays from a speaker.

When the trees clear, Ben is sitting at a table with three chairs in the middle of a framed house. Sitting next to him is Clayton. There's a vase of flowers in the middle—daisies, which I know symbolize his mom.

233

I try not to cry, but I lose the battle as the words of the song sink in. When I walk up the few stairs to get into the house, the music stops.

"Thanks for joining us," Ben says.

"Sit down, Mom." Clayton gestures to the empty chair.

I sit down.

"What do you think?" Ben looks around. "Enough room for us?"

"Um... yeah?"

Ben stands and gets a large rolled-up piece of paper from the floor beside him. He spreads it out on the table. It's the blueprint of the house, and on the top, it says "The Noughton/Adams Home."

I look at Clayton, and he nods.

"So, I'm thinking this is our bedroom since it overlooks the creek." Ben points out a room. "Does that seem good?"

I nod. "Sure." I can't say much more. I'm still so dumbstruck by what's happening right now.

"And I picked my room, Mom. As far away from you two as I could get." Clayton points at the blueprint. In his handwriting, it says, Clayton's room.

"He'll look over the lake, and the best part is that there's no way to sneak out."

I giggle, more tears trickling down my cheeks.

"But before we can have all this, you have to agree to something." Ben's gaze drinks me in.

I look to Clayton for guidance. "What?"

He nods to Ben, and I shift my focus back to him. He's on bended knee with a ring nestled snugly in a velvet pillow in a ring box.

"Gillian Adams, you've been my girl all of my life. I made a lot of stupid decisions that took me away from you. But I promise you, I'm done being stupid." Ben's head bobbles back and forth. "You might still have to keep me in line sometimes."

I laugh.

"Get on with it," Clayton says, rolling his eyes good-naturedly.

"If you marry me, I promise to always stand with you, dream with you, and love with you."

"What do you say, Mom?"

"You're okay with this?"

Clayton nods. "Ben and I had a talk."

"Oh, you did, did you?" I smile.

"So?" Ben asks.

"Was it even a real question? I'd love to be your wife. I've waited almost my whole life for this."

He takes the ring out and slides it on my finger. It's a perfect fit.

Ben urges me up and wraps me in his arms—the safest place in this world. His lips seek mine, and he kisses me. In that kiss, there are so many promises.

"Can we eat now? I'm starved," Clayton says.

We pull apart, and Ben slides his chair closer to me.

Jenson appears out of nowhere with a tray lined with covered dishes. "Congratulations." He lowers his head. "Enjoy your meal, because Emmett can't keep a secret. I'll keep them all at bay until after you eat."

We all chuckle.

"Thanks," Ben says, and I mouth "thank you," my voice not working. Ben raises his water glass. "Our first meal as a family."

Clayton raises his, and I lift mine. Our glasses meet in the middle of the table.

"Eventually she'll stop crying, right?" Clayton asks, and I laugh over a cry.

"Yeah, Clay, she will."

Sometimes dreams do come true, just years later and not how you expected.

A half hour passes before we're interrupted by the entire Noughton crew and Laurel and Sadie and of course Brooks. But I'd have it no other way. Clayton and I are finally home.

Epilogue

BEN

I knock on Gillian's door, and she opens it, laughing when she sees the bag in my hand.

"He kicked me out," I grumble.

She steps out of the way, and I walk inside. Clayton is busy in the kitchen.

"He kicked you out?" she asks.

"Said I'm an engaged man and should be living with my bride-to-be."

"And her son!" Clayton shouts.

"He wants you to live in sin?" She laughs.

I drop my bag.

She stares at the bag, then up at me. "Bedroom, Noughton."

"Does she always run a tight ship, Clay?"

He turns away from the stove, a plate of cookies in his hand. "She barks a lot, but if you guilt her, she'll pick up your stuff."

"Clay!" Gillian admonishes.

"Yeah, I think that's only for her kids. I'm not going to get the same treatment." I reach for a cookie that looks suspiciously like the ones Laurel sells.

Clayton slaps my hand. "That's for Kait."

I rock my head back and sneak a peek at Gillian, who smiles and says, "She's coming over to hang out, so you and I are stuck in the bedroom."

"Do you think I'm going to complain about that?" I wink at her.

"No!" Clayton says. "I better not hear any noises out of that room."

We both laugh, and I grab Gillian by the waist, pretending to maul her neck. She can't stop laughing, and Clayton keeps sighing as if we're the biggest losers in the world.

Our house isn't close to being done, but it will be before winter hits. My dad finally let me hire people to make the process faster. Said he was worried about the safety of Gillian and Clayton if I finished it myself. I still go over there and help the workers. The foreman doesn't understand why, but my dad was right. Something about building your own house for your family feels good.

Gillian accepted a position with the lawyer in Hickory to do her new attorney training. From there she might start interviewing at firms in bigger cities. We're unsure where the future will take us, and I'm not going to rush her to make a decision. I'll follow her wherever she wants to go.

The doorbell rings, and we scurry into the bedroom, laughing the entire way. Gillian opens the bedroom door slightly to listen in.

"Give him some space." I unpack my bag and shove some of my clothes into the drawers Gillian's already emptied for me.

Yeah, my dad kicked me out, but we'd already talked about living together. With Clayton.

"Hey, I wanted to talk to you about something," I say.

"Is it the football fundraiser we were supposed to be working on last night?"

"That was your fault. If you weren't so hot, I could've kept my hands to myself."

She laughs and lies on the bed, tempting me again.

"I want to call a family meeting."

"For?"

"The keypad."

She's quiet. "How do you know the keypad code?"

I put one knee on the bed and crawl to her. "Because someone was drunk and told me. I'm smart, you know, so I figured out the date. Tell me, fiancée, why is your key code the day I left for Clemson?"

She nibbles on her cheek, and I hover over her, waiting for her answer.

"It was a reminder."

"Of?"

"How much you hurt me. I changed it when you came back to town."

"That makes a lot of sense why you couldn't remember it when you were drunk. It was new."

She nods. "You waited all this time to bring it up?"

I bend down and kiss her neck. "I wanted to win you back before I brought it up. I wanted to make sure we had a new date." I kiss the other side of her neck. "So, I'm asking if we can use the date of our first family dinner?"

Her fingernails run through my hair. "I'll put it on the agenda. You'll need two out of the three votes." She cringes as though I might not get them.

My fingers fall to her ribs, tickling her. She screams, and I cover her mouth as she squirms to get away from my hands.

A knock hits the door. "Come on, guys. This is embarrassing."

"Sorry, Clay!" we say at the same time, our eyes locking.

My hands are sliding up her shirt just as my phone goes off. I let it go, but it rings again.

"Go see what it is," she says, sitting up in the bed we'll share tonight.

I grab my cell. "Jude," I say, sliding my thumb over the screen. "What's up?"

Jude delivers news I wasn't expecting to hear.

"Okay, we'll be right there." I put my phone in my pocket.

Gillian sits up straighter, seeing the expression on my face. "What is it?"

"Sadie's dad died."

"Oh no." Her hands go to her mouth.

"It's worse. She just got a notice of sale too. Apparently, her dad hasn't been paying the mortgage."

It's not a total surprise. Everyone knows Sadie's family farm hasn't been doing well. It's smaller and therefore harder to turn a profit. But I don't think anyone knew it was this bad.

"Oh my god, that's terrible." She frowns. "Let me cut this date thing short so we can go."

I sigh. "I hate doing that to him."

"He'll understand. It's family."

I nod, still feeling guilty for Clayton. Gillian walks out of the room, and a text message dings on my phone.

> Mark my words, they're engaged by the end of next season.

> Have some respect, her dad just died.

> Which is why things between them are about to change. I just wanted it out there that I'm calling it.

> Noted. Asshole.

> Wanting my brother to find love? I only
> want the best for you monogamous idiots.

> One day. Mark my words. I'm calling it.

> You're going to lose, brother.

Gillian walks into the room. "Come on, let's go. This is why I'll be happy when we're on the ranch." She walks back out of the room.

Sometimes I wonder how I got so lucky to win her twice. Mom must be looking out for me.

The End

No one in Willowbrook believes Jude and Sadie are just best friends. Are they right? Read Jude and Sadie's story to find out what breaks the thread from friends to lovers.

Learn more about The One I Stood Beside at
www.piperrayne.com

My Almost Ex

My Vegas Groom

A Greene Family Summer Bash (Novella)

My Sister's Flirty Friend

My Unexpected Surprise

My Famous Frenemy

A Greene Family Vacation (Novella)

My Scorned Best Friend

My Fake Fiancé

My Brother's Forbidden Friend

A Greene Family Christmas (Novella)

Lake Starlight

The Problem with Second Chances

The Issue with Bad Boy Roommates

The Trouble with Runaway Brides

The Drawback of Single Dads

Modern Love

Charmed by the Bartender

Hooked by the Boxer

Mad about the Banker

Single Dads Club

Real Deal

Dirty Talker

Sexy Beast

Holiday Romances

Single and Ready to Jingle

Claus and Effect

Cockamamie Unicorn Ramblings

And there you have it. The first book (prequel not included) in our new small town series! We hope you loved everything we love to include. The big family, the nosy town people, the special spots...

Our readers always love to pull secondary characters out of our books who they want to have a happy ever after. Ben Noughton first came on the page in the bonus scene of My Famous Frenemy (Greene Family #6) which earned him a bigger role in My Scorned Best Friend (Greene Family #7). After My Scorned Best Friend was released, we started getting emails and messages saying, "What about Ben?"

Then we had an opportunity to be a part of an anthology and we thought, "Let's write Ben's story!" It'll be a short and sweet novella (now the prequel One Last Summer) where readers can see him as a teen headed off to college. We deliberately set that story up to be a second chance romance so we could write a ranch series and give Ben his well-deserved HEA.

Of course, we had to go back to the prequel to change a few names and add some more details after we wrote The One I Left Behind, so if you have the original copy of the anthology, you may notice some changes. You all know by now we write ourselves into corners. This time it was nice to be able to change the prequel *before* we released it, setting up the Plain Daisy Ranch series perfectly. Well... as perfect as we can make it.

We love our big families in Alaska. And we love our towns Lake Starlight and Sunrise Bay, but it was refreshing to write in a brand-new world and discover again how certain characters pop off the page that you didn't realize would. Brooks for one. Emmett for another.

Things that changed from plotting to page—Clayton's dad was originally going to blackmail Ben and the black moment changed (literally two days before the deadline we were brainstorming back and forth). We added Gillian's dream to be a lawyer (during plotting we never gave her an exterior goal—she can't be ALL about her man. LOL). And there are probably so many more we're forgetting!

We gave you some glimpses into some books ahead and left you some Easter eggs to discover. Did you see them? We're excited and hope you are too to dive into this family series, and we can confirm that every cousin will get their own book because we love this family too much to say goodbye after the Noughton brothers!

As always, we have a lot of people to thank for getting this book into your hands...

Nina and the entire Valentine PR team.
Cassie from Joy Editing for line edits who is probably really surprised we got her the book on time! LOL
Ellie from My Brother's Editor for line edits and proofing.
Hang Le for the cover and branding for the entire series which is BEYOND beautiful in our opinion.
Regina Wamba for the beautiful photo, giving us the inspiration of Ben and Gillian.
All the bloggers who graciously carve out time to read, review and/or promote us.
All the Piper Rayne Unicorns who give us a fun space online to chat and show us love on the daily!
Readers – With so many books out there, we're so thankful

you've chosen ours. We hope we won you over with this first book in the series!

Jude Noughton? Our grumpy older brother has more heart than we originally thought. Anyone else cry during the visit to their mom's grave? He's been blind to what's been in front of him all these years and his best friend, Sadie Wilkins might just be done waiting around for him to notice her.

xo,

Piper & Rayne

About Piper & Rayne

Piper Rayne is a *USA Today* Bestselling Author duo who write "heartwarming humor with a side of sizzle" about families, whether that be blood or found. They both have e-readers full of one-clickable books, they're married to husbands who drive them to drink, and they're both chauffeurs to their kids. Most of all, they love hot heroes and quirky heroines who make them laugh, and they hope you do, too!

.